T0131336

THE AMBASSADOR TO BRAZIL

A NOVEL

PETER HORNBOSTEL

FOUR WINDS
— PRESS —

SAN FRANCISCO

Four Winds Press
San Francisco, CA

ISBN: 978-1-940423-11-1

Cover and interior design by Domini Dragoone

9 8 7 6 5 4 3 2 1

Distributed by Publishers Group West

for Susan
and Monika

PREFACE

In mid-March 1964, a secret task force of United States warships and tankers set sail from the Caribbean bound for Brazil. The flotilla, which had the code name "Brother Sam," included the world's largest aircraft carrier, several destroyers, a troop carrier and three tankers. The United States later claimed that it was only intended to "show the American flag," not invade, and that no one in the Brazilian military knew the task force was coming. In fact, neither was true. Although the flotilla never arrived in Brazilian waters, its actual purpose was to provide logistic and tactical support to the generals who were planning the coup. Of course they knew it was coming.

There were many in the United States government who were anxious to participate in the coup. The CIA was desperately seeking a way to resurrect its reputation, which had been shattered a few years earlier in the Bay of Pigs invasion of Cuba. Lincoln Gordon, the United States ambassador in Rio, a former Harvard professor, had achieved nothing by the embassy's surreptitious contributions of millions of dollars to the political campaigns of right wing Brazilian politicians. He was anxious for the United States to achieve some kind of success that he could claim as his own. Meanwhile, the White House was seeking to establish President Lyndon Johnson as leader of the hemisphere, in place of John Kennedy, whose reputation in death remained far greater than Johnson's own.

Although 50 years have passed since the "revolution to restore democracy" (as the CIA called it), much remains unknown about what the United States actually did, and what effect, if any, it had in bringing about the success of the coup. Declassified State Department cables have shed some light. Several CIA cables have also recently been declassified. But the operating cables that describe the activities of the Agency in Brazil remain classified. Presumably they contain information that the CIA prefers to keep secret, such as plans it may have had for the assassination of President Joao Goulart (as happened to President Allende in Chile several years later), the identity of its agents in Brazil, and details regarding Operation Brother Sam and its schedule.

Another question that has been completely buried is the risk of nuclear war between the United States and the Soviet Union triggered by Operation Brother Sam. The flotilla set sail less than two years after the Cuban missile crisis, at a time when Nikita Kruschev was still in power. The question is not mentioned in any publicly released United States government document.

In this work of fiction, Peter Hornbostel, legal advisor to USAID in Washington and Brazil from 1963 to 1968, tells the story of what the role of the United States may have been. Ambassador Anthony Carter, the protagonist of the book, was kept in the dark by the CIA regarding much of what was going on. The same may have happened to the actual US ambassador at the time, Lincoln Gordon. Gordon may not have known who was actually in charge of the CIA's operations in Brazil. Neither did Carter.

US President Lyndon Johnson, Brazilian Marshal Castelo Branco, and the Brazilian generals (Costa e Silva, Kruel, Geisel, Golbery, and others) were, of course, alive and well at the time of the coup. However, all words, actions, expressions, or intentions of any character are entirely fictional.

This is also a love story. Marina, Ambassador Carter's mistress is, of course, fictional as well. What a pity. . . .

—P.A.H.

CHAPTER 1

It's the rains of March
ending the summer;
It's the promise of life
in your heart.

—Vinicius de Moraes & Antonio Carlos Jobim,
"Aguas de Março"

Anthony Theodore Carter, ambassador of the United States of America to the Federative Republic of Brazil, nude but for the towel around his waist, stood at the window watching the rain which had been falling on Rio de Janeiro for six days, so hard now that he could barely see the buildings across Siqueira Campos Street through the rain. Three stories down, the rain had turned the street into a brown torrent, which raced down, across Rua Barata Ribeiro and Avenida Copacabana, over Avenida Atlantica, and then across the beach to the sea, itself turned brown by the rain.

Rio in the rain is not so marvelous, he thought to himself. "Cidade Maravilhosa." The Marvelous City. That was the name it was given by the Mangueira Samba School in the Carnaval parade a few years ago. It *is* marvelous, he thought, but not in the rain.

The first time he had seen Rio had been twenty years ago. It was summer, no rain, and Rio was full of light and life, and heat, and sex, and smells, not separately, but all mixed together under a blue tropical sky. His prop-driven Pan Am plane had emerged from the clouds, and he could see the green of the mountains, then the blue-gray of Guanabara Bay embracing the city. As the plane dropped lower, he could also see the slums—the shacks perched on poles above the sewage-dirty water along the edges of the bay. Ahead stood the peak of Corcovado with the famous statue of Christ, and the escarpment plunging down from the statue into the south zone of Rio where the elite lived, out of sight of the shanties along the bay. But all of it, even the shantytowns, looked colorful, even picturesque from the sky, although he knew they weren't.

The plane landed and rolled over to the terminal, a large white building with a balcony one floor up that was full of people. A large sign announced the airport as Galeão. Two brawny airport employees, their sweaty black bodies gleaming in the sun, rolled a mobile staircase over to the door of the plane. He was first in the line to disembark, and when the doors opened and Rio de Janeiro hit him square in the face, his eyes squinted almost shut against the glare of the concrete apron and the white of the terminal. On the balcony of the terminal, a five-person family was shouting a samba, somewhat off-key, while the littlest boy banged out the rhythm on a makeshift tin drum. His two older brothers were holding a welcome home sign reading *Bem vinda Mariazinha!,* Welcome home little Maria. Dozens of other families crowded the balcony, craning their necks and shouting to the passengers streaming by them below, laden with shopping bags and boxes, on their way to customs.

But what he remembered most clearly was the air that swept into the plane, displacing the stale air of the fourteen-hour journey from Washington. It seemed to be at least 90 degrees and humid as a steam bath. And it smelled—well, it smelled like Rio de Janeiro. He had tried again and again to sort out the ingredients of that smell: Clearly it included jet fuel, human sweat, and jasmine, plus another flower he did not know. And there was the water of the bay at the end of the runway, a cool fresh breeze with a whiff of sewage, but only now and then. Coffee definitely. And bananas. And oranges, or was it pineapple? Cigarette smoke. They all blended together, like the colors of a rainbow.

He walked under the balcony into a terminal which looked like a movie set. The ceiling of the main hall, three stories high, was held up by a number of huge columns some four feet in diameter. He wouldn't have been a bit surprised if Alec Guinness, dressed in a white suit, had popped out from behind one of them. People everywhere—their skins every shade of white, brown and black. And, of course, the hum of Portuguese, and radios, and taxis along the side of the terminal that was wide open to the street.

Although he was only a Class 3 Foreign Service officer back then, the embassy had sent a car and a secretary to meet him. The moment he got into the air-conditioned car, which seemed to be hermetically sealed against the world outside, the smells of Rio vanished, to be replaced by the acrid-sweet smell of American disinfectant. The young Foreign Service officer sent to meet him had remained in the cool of the car.

"Sorry about not getting out," he said. "Too damn hot out there . . . and smelly. Did you have a good trip, sir?"

"Just fine," he replied.

"You've been to Rio before?"

He was not interested in diplomat chitchat. "I think I'll rest a bit," he said. He leaned back and closed his eyes down to narrow slits; he hoped his escort could not see that they were still slightly open. "Wake me up when we get there," he said.

The car drove through what looked like a light industrial zone, which also contained a surprising number of motels with names like Love Nest, King and Queen, Pussy Cat, and one called Aspen, with a large billboard showing a bundled up person heading downhill on what the artist must have thought skis looked like. Why so many motels, he mused, and why out here?

After half an hour, the factories, warehouses, and motels gave way to apartment houses and small shops, until the road emerged onto the shore of Guanabara Bay. Now they were speeding along a road skirting the bay, in front of the old elegant apartment houses that looked out onto it. In the background towered Sugarloaf, the huge gray-brown rock formation with a red cable car running up it, which appeared in every picture book he had ever seen about Brazil.

The car ducked through a pair of short tunnels and then out onto Avenida Atlantica and the beach. The beach was wide—perhaps fifty meters of white sand between the Avenue and the blue of the sea. Closer to the ocean, he could see the sun worshippers, some sitting under umbrellas, others stretched out on the sand, still others standing around and talking or playing volleyball. They stopped for a traffic light. In front of the car, dozens of beautiful tanned bodies—mostly young girls in their teens—walked across the avenue on their way to or from the beach. One, a lovely brown-skinned girl in a scanty bikini, looked into the car and smiled.

Carter's escort officer nudged him. "We're at your hotel," he said. The hotel was a large white structure, dripping with Victorian ornamentation, facing the sea. A bronze plaque by the side of the front door read "Hotel Copacabana Palace 1886." A dark-skinned liveried doorman opened the door to the car. "Welcome to Rio, sir." he said with a perfect English accent. "Did you have a good flight . . . ?"

From the sidewalk behind the car, a beggar with no legs, on a plywood platform with rollers, scooted over to the car. The doorman shooed him away.

That was twenty years ago. In the meantime, he had been posted to Cairo, Portugal, Kenya, Ecuador, and one tour in Washington on the Brazil

Desk. The "Desk" was not just a desk, but about twenty of them crowded into two large offices on the third floor at State, manned by thirty or more young Foreign Service officers who thought they were making the foreign policy of the United States. They reported to the head of the Brazil Desk, who reported to the assistant secretary of state for inter-American affairs, who reported to the secretary of state, who reported to the president of the United States. Carter had become an expert at shuffling incoming cables to the right officer within the State Department, and correcting the spelling and syntax of outgoing cables before they were sent. After two years of bureaucratic labor at the Desk, the department had finally rewarded him with the title of United States ambassador to Brazil. Priscilla and he had celebrated with dinner at Rive Gauche. It was the best restaurant in Georgetown. Priscilla was ecstatic. "Oh Tony," she said, "it's going to be such fun!"

It had not been such fun for her, Carter mused. It wasn't really fair. It was all so different now.

Behind him, from the dark of the apartment, he heard the sheets of the bed rustling.

"You're up," Marina said.

He nodded.

"Is it still raining?"

"Sure," he said, "it's going to rain forever."

"Well, then, come back to bed."

"I can't. I have to go to the embassy. It's my job to be there. There's going to be a coup—a revolution—and it's going to happen soon. I have to go."

She got up from the bed and walked over to where he stood by the window. She was tall, slim, with soft light brown Brazilian skin, full, perfectly shaped breasts with dark brown nipples, long straight black hair, and incredible gray-green eyes. She brought her nude body up against his and with one hand fiddled with the towel around his waist.

"Whose revolution is it?" she asked. "Is it *your* revolution?"

"No," he said.

"Well then, there's no hurry about going, is there?" she said. She fiddled a little more and the towel slid to the floor. She looked down at him approvingly. "Oh come on," she said.

It was hopeless to argue.

Outside, in the rain, a black 1949 Plymouth sedan was slowly weaving its way down the brown torrent that used to be Siqueira Campos street, around the empty banana boxes, destroyed furniture, old tires, and other detritus washed down from the slum on the hill by the rain. The car slowed, then stopped in front of the building. The driver, a swarthy bald Brazilian with a brownish-gray complexion, opened his window, pulled out a pair of binoculars, and scanned the face of the building. There was a window open on the third floor, but no one was there. The driver cursed softly. Then he took out a camera with a long lens and, although the American ambassador was not to be seen, he snapped a photo of the open window and drove on, disappearing into the rain. The ambassador was out of sight in the back of the room, otherwise engaged.

CHAPTER 2

Carter had first seen her at a reception at the Romanian embassy. It had been another of those goddamn National Day cocktail parties. One hundred fifteen countries plus the Vatican were diplomatically represented in Brazil. That meant 115 ambassadors plus the Papal Nuncio. Of course, all of them except the Vatican had Independence Days. That was to be expected. But eighty-seven of them also had National Days, on which they would have parties as well. He had long since stopped going to these, until the foreign ministry of the government of Malta (he hadn't even known that Malta was a country) complained to Washington that he hadn't attended their National Day party. The idiots on the Brazil Desk sent a cable instructing him that "it is the policy of the United States that all ambassadors attend all National Day parties of countries accredited to the countries in which they were located if that is the host country." At first he couldn't quite figure out what the cable meant, and so decided to ignore it. Besides, since when did the Desk establish the policy of the United States? But he had to pick his fights with Washington carefully these days, so in the end he went along. Whenever he could, he sent his deputy chief of mission, Maurice A. Villepringle, in his place. Villepringle even liked those goddamn parties. But the DCM was on a reconnaissance trip to Recife in Northeast Brazil, and so Carter had gone himself.

Now he stood off to the side of the hall at the brand new Romanian embassy building, holding a champagne glass of seltzer into which he had squeezed a tiny drop of the yellow Easter-egg dye, which turned the bubbly water a pale yellow.

"So you like our champagne?" the third secretary of the Romanian embassy asked. "Frankly, I think it's far superior to the French, don't you?"

Carter assured him that he agreed.

"Oh, I'm so glad," said the Romanian. He noticed someone across the hall. "Oh, there's Ambassador Sverdlov. I'm afraid I must speak to him for just a moment. Please excuse me," and he hurried off.

Carter looked around the hall. His host, the young Romanian ambassador, was chatting with Sverdlov, the Russian ambassador, who was looking particularly grumpy, even for him. Red drapes had been hung on the walls, together with a large photograph of Ceauşescu, and a few pictures of smiling Romanian children reading small red books, apparently with great pleasure. All the usual suspects chattered with each other in small groups around the room, clutching glasses of Romanian champagne. Several were holding similar small, red leather-bound books. He spotted Jack Sprague, the medic at the Canadian embassy, and walked over. Jack was one of his few real friends in the Rio diplomatic corps.

"Well, Mr. Ambassador, what a pleasant surprise to see you here," said Sprague. "Isn't it a lovely party?" Dr. Sprague knew Washington's instructions about attending National Day parties.

"Fuck you," said Carter.

"Oh, come on. I know you love these things. And the food is so delicious." He snared a nasty-looking pastry from a passing tray. "Have one or two of these," he said. "After that you'll need my medical services, and you won't be so disrespectful."

Carter laughed.

"I guess Villepringle is out of town," said Sprague, "or I wouldn't be having the pleasure of your company, right?"

"Right."

"So, what's new?" said Sprague. "You guys still trying to get the generals to kick this booby president out of office? Or are you gonna do it yourselves? Not that I blame you, you understand."

Carter was appalled. How did Sprague know that the CIA was advising the Brazilian military on the best strategy for "kicking out" the Goulart government, and "saving democracy" in Brazil? Some of the spooks even believed that the United States should do the job itself, to make sure it was done right. He wasn't sure what they meant by "right." Nor that they could do the job better than the Brazilians, whatever "right" meant.

"Jack, you know better," he said. "The United States would never support any kind of military uprising against a democratically elected government, or interfere in the domestic sovereignty of any other country." Carter realized how stuffy he must sound, but this was what he was supposed to say.

"Oh sure," said Sprague. "What about Santo Domingo? Or Haiti? Or Panama?"

But Carter didn't hear him. He was staring across the room at a tall, slender, brown-skinned young woman with gray-green eyes wearing a demure black dress who was moving in their direction, passing out little red leather-covered books, which looked just like the books that held the rapt attention of the children in the pictures on the walls. "Look at that," he breathed to Sprague.

"Wow," said the doctor, "I'd like to examine *her*. I know Brazilian mulattas are gorgeous, but this one. . . . " He paused. "You're the United States ambassador, Tony, and you're a married man. You can't screw around like I can."

"This is Rio de Janeiro," said Carter, "anything goes here."

"I know," said Sprague softly. "But you're not a Brazilian, you're American and you're still a married man. And you are Mr. Ambassador."

The girl was, by now, standing in front of them. She smiled, "I'd like to offer you gentlemen copies of the new book written by our beloved President Ceauşescu. It contains a brilliant exposition on the Romanian peasant, and his role in the glorious socialist revolution in Romania." She had obviously memorized her little speech.

"What is a gorgeous *carioca* like you doing passing out Communist propaganda for the Romanian embassy?" Carter asked in Portuguese.

The girl remained silent.

"You haven't answered my question," Carter said. He realized that he was again sounding like a stuffy striped-pants diplomat. "You are very beautiful," he added.

Her face darkened into a blush; the smile remained in place. "You already have a copy?" she said. "I'm so glad." And she moved gracefully on to repeat her pitch to the Moroccan chargé d'affaires, who was standing a few steps further on.

"Now, that was innocent enough, wasn't it, Jack?"

"Yes, Mr. Ambassador," said Sprague, a grin on his face.

"You know, Jack," Carter said. "I don't think I've ever seen a girl that beautiful before."

CHAPTER 3

Actually, he had. Just before Carnaval, Gabriel Ferreira, General Counsel of AMFORP, the American-Foreign Power Company, had invited Carter and Priscilla to watch the Carnaval parade on Saturday night from AMFORP's offices on the Avenida Presidente Vargas. "It's better for you, Mr. Ambassador," Ferreira said, "air-conditioned, safe, not so smelly." The Carters quickly accepted.

The parade had already started when he and Priscilla arrived. "Don't worry," Ferreira said in his perfect English, "you haven't missed much. And the parade goes on until tomorrow morning at four. Then it'll pick up again at eight. Would you like a whiskey? A caipirinha, perhaps? Of course, we have soft drinks for the wives, too," he said, looking at Priscilla.

Carter looked around the room. Several foreign businessmen were there. He nodded across the room to the vice president of First National City Bank. Hans Klaus, president of Volkswagen do Brasil, was chatting in the corner with another gringo Carter didn't know. The president of General Electric had brought a beautiful Brazilian girl, clearly not his spouse. There were no other Brazilians. All but the girl were foreigners.

Carter grinned at his host. "Don't you Brazilians do Carnaval?" he asked. "Only us gringos?"

"Well," Ferreira answered, "it depends on which Brazilians. Carnaval is the people's holiday, not ours. It's only four and a half days, once a year. They deserve at least that. So we get out of their way. We go to our summer places in Petropolis or Terespolis, or Buzios . . . ."

"But I don't get it," Carter said. "Thousands of Americans come to Rio every year, just to see the Carnaval parade."

"Are you sure that's all they come for?"

Carter looked puzzled.

"Look," Ferreira said, "have I ever told you my definition of Carnaval?"

Carter nodded no.

"Well," Ferreira said, looking over to the window. "To me Carnaval is that time of year when thousands of fools try desperately, under impossible conditions, to do what it is so easy to do here the rest of the year under ideal conditions." He smiled. "So I leave," he added, "except when I must be here to host this little party. But that's a pleasure, of course."

"That's very gracious of you," Carter said.

The glass in the windows had begun to rattle, and Carter could hear the samba beat of a new group of drummers making their way down the avenue. "Come look," Ferreira said, making his way to the window. "That's what *you* are here for, after all, even if some of your countrymen are looking for something else."

Nine black drummers dressed in shimmering green costumes had stopped in front of the building and were firmly hammering out a samba rhythm. A younger man, somewhat lighter in color, danced nearby playing a large tambourine. Another was passing a short stick over what seemed to be some kind of wooden tube. Another was playing a tambourine. There were no other musical instruments. The audience was enthusiastically singing a samba. Swirling around the drums were several hundred dancers, their skins of every shade of brown and black, dancing to the music of the drums. Many of them were dressed in glistening costumes apparently made of green and purple rayon, spotted with shiny golden stars. Several of the male dancers had giant golden wings attached to their shoulders. Everyone was beautifully costumed.

In the midst of the dancers, a float moved slowly down the avenue. It looked to Carter something like a wedding cake with a pier sticking out the front. On the first layer, a number of dancers, more skilled than those on the avenue, swirled gracefully in and out of each other's arms to the rhythm of the drums. On the pier, a slim couple dressed in formal attire of purple and green danced a complex set of samba steps.

On the next level up, four scantily clad young women swayed at the centers of four large silver stars marked N, O, S, and L, which, Carter assumed, stood for north, west, south, and east. A giant gold column rose from the center of the second level to support the smaller third level on which a beautiful brown-skinned girl stood, waving regally to the crowd. She was dressed only in a long shimmering tail of blue-green fabric covered with small blue mirrors. Her breasts were bare.

"That's the Bangu Samba School," Ferreira said. "They won the Carnaval competition last year."

"I'm not surprised," Carter replied.

"She's Yemanja," Ferreira added, nodding to the float, "the fish-tailed Goddess of the Sea. Perhaps our most important goddess. All of us in Rio respect her, even those who don't practice Macumba."

Carter looked puzzled.

"Macumba is based mostly on African religions." Ferreira went on, "It is practiced by a lot of our people who are poorer and of African descent. Not many wealthier people are followers. But many of us go down to the beach on New Year's Eve, when Yemanja is said to pass closest to shore, and throw flowers into the surf, just to cover our bets."

"If that's what she looks like," Carter said, "I'd throw flowers, too."

CHAPTER 4

Carter had a total of three cars. The car for official occasions was a black 1955 Cadillac, complete with fixtures on the front bumper where he could attach small American flags if he wanted, and curtains on the side to hide the identity of whoever was inside. It came with a driver named Joaozinho. Joaozinho had a large mustache and a chauffeur's cap, which he wore whenever he drove Carter anywhere, about once a week. The rest of the time he spent shining up the car and otherwise doing *"porra nenhuma"* (Portuguese for "nothing at all").

His second car was a deep maroon Aero Willys. It was one of the only two cars being manufactured in Brazil, and about as uncomfortable as a car could get. The springs seemed to be solid steel, the seats hard and angled so that they put your feet to sleep within minutes. As far as he could tell, there were no shock absorbers. The engine noise resembled the sound of a Sherman tank rumbling down Avenida President Vargas. It had been given to the embassy by a distant and clearly anti-American member of the Willys family, and was used only when the United States wanted, for one reason or another, to show off its use of products made in Brazil. Fortunately, that wasn't too often.

His favorite car by far was his VW beetle, or Fusca, as the Brazilians called it, painted yellow with a discreet dark blue stripe down the side. It had been a taxi until a year ago when Carter bought it used from a local taxi company. He persuaded the sales manager to throw in an electrified sign that read "Taxi", which he could attach to the top of the car with a couple of bungee cords. Usually, though, that wasn't necessary. He could achieve almost complete anonymity simply by driving it through the streets of Rio de Janeiro, which contained thousands of other Fuscas just like it.

He was glad to be driving it now, on his way to the embassy. While the car was small, the motor in the back of the car was fairly high above the chassis, and the spark plugs were located near the top of that. Siqueira Campos crossed Barata Ribeiro a few hundred meters down the street, where the water had formed a brown lake. He stopped at the edge of it.

Carter knew all about this lake. And the others like it. The storm sewers were clogged up all over Rio de Janeiro, and had been for years. He had offered the municipal government some American sewer-cleaning equipment, and to have USAID finance a project to rebuild the storm sewers in Copacabana. That was a year ago, and Washington was still trying to figure out whether the government of the State of Guanabara, which covered exactly the same area as the City of Rio de Janeiro, was really for or against the national government of President Joao Goulart, and whether the project should therefore be disapproved or approved. The problem was that although Carlos Lacerda, the governor of the State of Guanabara, was vehemently opposed to the Goulart government, the mayor of the city seemed to be in favor.

Per instructions from Washington, the political section at the embassy kept two lists, the A list and the B list, of the various political subdivisions and governmental bodies of Brazil: ministries, the armed forces, states, municipalities, territories, agencies, divisions, government-owned corporations, etc. The A list were the "democratic forces" arrayed against the Goulart government. The B list were his "pinko" supporters. All AID financed projects were to be directed exclusively to the political bodies and politicians on the A list, never to those on the B list. In the case of Rio de Janeiro, the state of Rio de Janeiro was on the A list; the city of Rio de Janeiro was on the B list. But both covered exactly the same geographic area.

The storm sewer problem was further complicated by the fact that although the sewers themselves were under the jurisdiction of the state water and sewer authority (clearly A list), the streets and the sewer grates were a municipal responsibility, and hence on the B list. Stoney Wyndam, the USAID sewer engineer who was blissfully ignorant even of the existence of the A and B lists or of any political issues at all, had prepared a proposal for rebuilding the storm sewers and sent it to the ambassador. In the hope of slipping it through the bureaucracy if it were called a "study" (the State Department loved studies), Carter had retitled the project as a "Study Proposal", and sent it to Washington for approval and authorization.

But now, a year later, the bureaucrats in Washington were still studying Stoney's proposal. The Desk was simply unable to deal with a project which was on the A list and the B list at the same time, and so Carter was now faced with a small brown lake at the corner of Barata Ribeiro and Siqueira Campos, wondering whether his VW beetle would make it through.

"Oh, what the hell," he said out loud. Carter put the car in gear, and very slowly started through the lake. It did not take long for the water to reach the hubcaps. A few seconds later, it was starting to seep into the car at the bottom of the door. He inched forward. Now the water reached the headlights. He thought he could feel the car begin to float; if it did, he thought, maybe the spark plugs would stay above water. Not likely, though. And then, just as he was certain the motor was bound to die, he could feel the tires take hold, and begin to pull the car out of the lake on the other bank and back onto Rua Barata Ribeiro.

"Well, Mr. Ambassador," he said to himself, "You're out of hot water one more time." Chuckling at his own joke, he drove on through the pelting rain toward the center of the city, and the United States embassy. Two blocks from Siqueira Campos, a 1949 black Plymouth sedan pulled out of Rua Santa Clara, and followed him as far as Flamengo, where it turned off onto Rua Paissandu and disappeared. Carter did not notice it.

CHAPTER 5

One thing he hated about the job of ambassador was that it set you apart from and above almost everyone else on the social pecking order. Not that he minded that inside the embassy he was chief of mission and head of the country team. Theoretically that put him above even the spooks, at least when he knew what they were up to. But he hated being "Mr. Ambassador" to the Brazilians, especially those who were not in the foreign ministry. He would have liked to joke with taxi drivers rather than riding in his aging Cadillac with the embassy driver. He thought about trading good-natured insults with the waiters at the Bar Lagoa, rather than sitting at state dinners making small talk with the wife of some African ambassador. He would have liked to play chess with the old timers at Posto 6 at the end of the Copacabana Beach. But the ambassador of the most powerful nation on earth could not be seen doing these things.

Soon after he had arrived in Rio, a young man from the American School asked for a brief appointment. Curious, Carter agreed. It seemed the school was setting up a drama department as well as a small English-language theater. The young man, who was to be the drama teacher, had heard that the ambassador had done some acting in college. Would he be willing to give a short talk at the opening of the theater before the first performance?

"I'd be delighted," said Carter. "But there's one condition." The young man's face clouded. "I'd also like to be in your play, just a bit part. Do you think you could handle that?"

The young man's face turned from clouds to summer sunshine. "That would be wonderful, Mr. Ambassador, just wonderful."

And so Carter wound up playing the butler in *The Man Who Came to Dinner,* the first play ever produced by the Little Theater of Rio de Janeiro. At the last rehearsal (he missed most of the earlier ones), the idea came to him. "I think the part calls for a mustache," he told the stage manager. And because he was the ambassador, they hustled off and got him one.

That mustache had come in handy more than once. After a night working late at the embassy, he would sometimes drive out to one of the bars at the end of Copacabana Beach, and have a caipirinha by himself, unrecognized by anyone, far from the embassy and all the bureaucratic folderol. His favorite was the Bar Atlantico with its large outside terrace facing the sea, near where Avenida Atlantica turned the corner and headed toward Ipanema. The chess tables along the beach opposite were abandoned by the time he arrived. Pulled up on the beach next to them were several small fishing boats, all painted different colors. Carter was always surprised to see them there, in the middle of the second largest city in Brazil.

And now he sat at the back of the terrace outside of the Bar Atlantico behind Posto 6 on Copacabana Beach, enjoying his ice cold *chopp,* as the Brazilians called their tap beer. The mustache was firmly stuck on with theatrical gum. He was wearing horn-rimmed glasses in lieu of his usual contacts. And his hair was stuck onto his head with too much Brylcreem. He was afraid it looked a bit ridiculous, but there was no way anyone could recognize him. He hadn't taken that course in makeup in college for nothing.

"Hello, Mr. Ambassador," said a soft voice from behind him. "What are you doing here?"

He almost didn't recognize her. In place of the demure black cocktail dress she had worn at the Romanian embassy, she was now wearing a short pair of hot pants. Her platform shoes had heels higher than he had ever seen before. On top, she wore a black see-through blouse, cut low to accentuate her cleavage. Her mascara and lipstick were perfect. She was gorgeous.

"Mind if I sit down?" she said in Portuguese, as she sat down next to him and lit a cigarette. "Paulinho," she called out to the waiter, "Johnnie Walker Black on the rocks, please." She put her hand over his. "So, like I asked you, Tony, what are you doing here?" It was the first time that any woman other than Priscilla had addressed him by his first name since he arrived in Brazil.

He stared at her. "How did you know who I am?" he asked.

She laughed. "Men are my profession," she said. "It would be one big mess if I couldn't tell them apart. Besides," she added, "I don't run into many of them as handsome as you."

He knew it was just business flattery, but he liked it nonetheless.

"And your mustache is on crooked, too."

He reached up quickly but the gum had hardened it on. She laughed again, a mischievous twinkle in her eye. "Oh, I'm only kidding. I like to make things up," she said. "Not just my face."

The whiskey came; he ordered another *chopp*. "What were you doing at the Romanian embassy?" he asked.

"Oh, she said, "I was sleeping with Lamenski then. He's the Romanian ambassador . . . but I'm sure you know that. His secretary quit—the sex was terrible, he said, so I helped out a little, passing out the 'great leader's' book, and doing some other things." She stopped for a moment. "He was a nice man, Lamenski, I taught him a few things. He taught me a few things. But he ran out of money, at least that's what he said."

"You left him?"

"Sure," she said. "Love is nice, but I can't live on just love. The factory would go under."

"Factory?"

"Oh, I'm sure I could live on what I can make on the street," she continued. "I'm young and I'm beautiful, but that won't last forever. And then what?"

Carter was incredulous. "So you built yourself a factory for the day when you—"

She interrupted him. "Oh, it's just a little building near the favela in Bangu, with four sewing machines and four girls who sew for me. And there's a cutting table, too, and a guy who cuts for me. That's a lot of mouths to feed, to say nothing of the fabric we buy. And the ribbons. It's expensive, and the best terms I can get from my suppliers is thirty days. I don't get paid by my customers for ninety days. So I need working capital. Now, how many banks do you know who will lend to a girl with four sewing machines out in Bangu? Of course they won't. So I get my working capital on the street, which isn't so bad really."

How could prostitution be "not so bad," Carter thought. His public health people thought it was terrible, for both the community and for the prostitutes themselves. He was sure they were right. But he had heard that the Dutch and also the French didn't agree. Prostitution was legal there. He decided not to say anything.

"There are always a few assholes," she continued, "and a few pricks—figure of speech—but most of the clients are OK. A few of them actually wind up buying a sewing machine for me—in installments. I name the machine after them if they would like that."

She stopped. "Oh, I haven't even told you what we produce," she said. "We make children's clothes. Toddlers, really. It's a good business in Brazil. Lots of toddlers."

She paused again. "I'm sorry," she said. "I must be boring you. It's just I get so excited about my little factory."

Carter was amazed. A streetwalker with her own factory? Making clothes for toddlers? That couldn't happen in the United States. And if it did, no one would believe it. "No," he said. "It's fascinating."

"You mean it's fascinating that a streetwalker can have a factory as well?"

He didn't reply.

"Most of us are like that," she said. "I'm lucky. I've got my own business. A lot of the girls just have day jobs. They're bank tellers, secretaries, salespeople, waitresses, but you'll never get a life that way. So we find a way to make a little money on the side, or on the back, that will make life worth living."

"Most people get married," he said. Like Priscilla and me, he thought.

"Oh, lots of us have been married," she said. "But so many married men are such shits. They're not faithful, so why should we be? It's better to be on the street. At least as long as you're young and pretty.

"Enough of all of that," she said. "Come on, Mr. Ambassador, let's go somewhere." Under the table, she ran her hand up his leg and stopped at his crotch. He could feel himself getting hard, his breath coming a little bit faster. But he couldn't do this. He was a married man. American married men didn't sleep with streetwalkers.

"I can't do that, I'm a married man," he stammered.

She laughed. "Most of my clients are married. The single guys are young and sexy; they don't need us. But the married guys, sure they're getting it at home, but often it's not very good, or maybe they're not getting it at all. Regardless, I can tell you this: They're not happy. That's why they come to see me. . . . What about you, Mr. Ambassador? How's your sex life?"

Suddenly it was really urgent that he get away. "I've got to go," he said. "My wife is waiting . . . .Waiter," he called out. "Waiter, the check. Right away, please."

The check came out the equivalent of $39.60. The whiskeys were US$16 each, plus $2 each for the *chopp*, plus the mandatory ten percent tip.

"Paulinho, take off the whiskey," she said. The waiter hustled away and came back with a check for a total of $6.60. She smiled at

Carter. "It wasn't really whiskey, you know. Just strong tea. We get a cut on what they sell."

She took her hand out from under the table and ran it through his hair. "You can leave off the hair tonic next time," she said, "and the mustache, I'll know you anyway."

He got up. "What's your name?"

"Marina," she said. Her gray-green eyes locked onto his. "Ciao, Mr. Ambassador. Come see me. We'll have a cup of tea together." She grinned. "On the rocks."

He watched her walk down Copacabana Beach until she turned into Rua Siqueira Campos and disappeared from sight.

CHAPTER 6

Roberto Barbosa Vieira Filho had invited Carter to Sunday lunch at his mansion outside Petropolis. Roberto, although Brazil-born, was something of a polyglot: He had studied economics at Yale, held a doctorate in literature from the Sorbonne, and was married to a lovely Chilean woman named Celeste. Roberto was an accomplished classical pianist who played regularly at home and occasionally at dinner parties hosted by his friends in their elegant apartments facing the ocean in Ipanema. Carter liked him immensely.

Vieira was the managing director of Light, the Brazilian subsidiary of a Canadian company named Brazilian Traction, after the trolley system that ran through Santa Teresa to Corcovado, which the company built in the 1890s. The trolley itself was called the *bonde*, after the bond issue, the first in Brazil, that financed it. Light owned the power distribution grids in Rio and Sao Paulo, as well as the telephone network in Rio, which worked sporadically, if at all. He was also on the board of American Foreign Power Company—AMFORP.

"We could fix the phones, of course." Roberto had told Carter at lunch a few weeks earlier. "But the government hasn't allowed us a rate increase in four years. With inflation at more than 100%, we're losing our shirts. We get the blame for the terrible service, of course. You pick up the phone and you can't get a line. I've seen secretaries holding six phones to their ears at once waiting for a line. But it's not our fault, really. Until we get a rate increase, my shareholders won't let me invest one cruzeiro in new equipment. Our rates wouldn't even begin to pay for it. I can't blame them."

Like most of the Brazilian elite, Roberto had a weekend place near Petropolis, a small city in the mountains near Rio, where Dom Pedro II had once held sway as the emperor of both Portugal and Brazil, and where Dom Pedro IV, pretender to the Brazilian throne, still lived in a small apartment in a museum that had once been the imperial palace. The road to Petropolis from Rio snaked up the mountains in a series of hairpin turns, through a dense tropical forest, one of the last surviving bits of the Atlantic rain forest—the *mata Atlantica*—that once covered almost the entire coastal region of the state of Rio de Janeiro. Here and there, at primitive roadside stands made of bamboo, women sold large clusters of tiny bananas for next to nothing, and peasants walked barefoot down the road on their way, Carter imagined, to the city far below. The air from the forest grew cooler as the car drove higher, until the road flattened out at about 1000 meters above Rio, and the air was actually cold.

Joaozinho maneuvered the Cadillac through the narrow streets of Petropolis and on to Nogueira, a small town higher yet than Petropolis itself.

Roberto's nineteenth-century mansion was placed well behind a black wrought iron gate set in a tall pink wall. Through the gate, Carter could see a tropical garden with a line of towering royal palms, at least a dozen types of bromeliads, a profusion of orchids near the gate (collected, Carter knew, by Roberto himself), and several acres of manicured lawn. Joaozinho sounded the horn lightly, and the gate opened. They drove another 200 meters up the curved drive to the house. Roberto and Celeste were waiting at their beautifully carved jacaranda front door.

"Anthony, how good of you to come. And in such difficult times. I know how busy you must be. It is a treat to have you here." Roberto's English was perfect.

Roberto ushered him into the house. Carter had been in the house before: It was one of those wonderful understated combinations of money and good taste. On one side wall of the front hall hung a Di Cavalcanti, on the other a small Picasso. "Roberto," Carter said, "you are too generous, to give up a Sunday with your orchids and your lovely wife."

Vieira laughed. "But it is my pleasure," he said. "I hope you don't mind, we have invited Alfred Smith Barrington as well. You know him, of course."

"I'm afraid not," Carter said, "but I certainly know his name."

"Well, you're in for a treat. His name may be British but he is one hundred percent Brazilian. His family have been coffee planters and bankers in Sao Paulo for seven generations. Alfred is chairman of the Barrington Bank, and he flies his own plane. In fact, he's flying up specially to have lunch with us." Roberto was clearly pleased.

They were in Roberto's orchideum when Barrington arrived.

"No problem with the plane, I trust?" Roberto asked. "You're almost three minutes late." His eyes twinkled.

"Oh, Roberto," Celeste said, "you're always teasing poor Alfred just because his family is British. Or at least used to be."

"No problem with the plane," Barrington said. "I just got a little lost over Araras, but the resident birds showed me the way."

They all laughed. Araras was a town in the mountains near Petropolis named after the large colorful macaws that once lived there in profusion. Carter had a pair of them at the residence in Rio. The birds had been together for years, and were inseparable. Carter loved them.

"Well," Roberto said, "are we all ready for lunch? Or perhaps you'd like a whiskey first?"

Sunday lunch, as always in Brazil, included an overcooked dry pork roast, rice, beans, *chuchu*, and a beautiful cheese and vegetable soufflé. The wine was a 1959 Chambertin. The rice, beans, and soufflé were delicious, the roast pork virtually inedible, and the *chuchu* . . . well, it was *chuchu*. Carter had eaten some excellent dinners at Roberto's house. But Sunday lunch always included that overcooked, dried-out pork roast and the tasteless *chuchu*. It was obligatory. He wondered why. The wine, as always, was superb.

After lunch, Celeste withdrew and the men moved into the study for brandy and cigars. Business discussions at dinner were strictly forbidden in Brazil, but not over brandy and cigars. That, in fact, was what brandy and cigars were for, once the first snifter had been appreciated over more social matters.

Carter slipped his lips around the brown cigar and his mind drifted to Marina and her brown Brazilian body. And her breasts almost breaking out of her black blouse. But that body was not for him. He was the United States ambassador. This luncheon was the kind of work he was paid to do, not dreaming about a streetwalker.

"Anthony," Roberto said, "What is the United States likely to do if Goulart attempts to pull off a coup from the left?"

"You know I can't comment on that, Roberto," Carter said. "That is an international matter of the Federative Republic of Brazil. Besides, how in hell would I know? I'm only the ambassador, not the CIA."

Both Roberto and Barrington laughed.

"So, are you saying," Barrington interjected, "that there is nothing the United States will do to support the forces of democracy here?"

"Who do you mean by the 'forces of democracy?'" Carter asked. "The military?"

"Well, we can trust them to do the right thing," Barrington said. "Marshal Braga has said the military will turn the government over to the civilians as soon as the communists have been weeded out. A matter of a few weeks, maybe a month. Of course, you can never be sure."

Carter turned to Roberto. "Is Braga likely to be the next president if the coup comes off?" he asked.

"If we're lucky," Roberto said. "He's probably the best one out of the military lot." He paused for a moment. "It's really up to us Brazilians. There isn't much the United States government can do short of launching an invasion, and I'm sure you would never do that."

Carter looked quickly into Roberto's eyes, but found nothing there. "If Washington is planning an invasion, they haven't told me about it," he said. "And I doubt they would try anything like that without the ambassador being on board." At least I hope not, he thought.

"Well, the phone company is going to play its part," Roberto said. "This coup is not going to be fought out with tanks and guns. That's not the Brazilian way. In fact, I'll bet there won't be a shot fired. This coup is going to be negotiated on the telephone between the armies that support Goulart and those who don't, and whoever has the most troops is going to win! It will be sort of a game."

"But can't Jango do the same thing?" Carter asked.

"No," Roberto said. "Jango won't." He held his index finger to his lips to signal a secret. "Because when the coup begins, we are going to cut off phone service to the Laranjeiras Palace, but we'll leave the trunk lines between the generals open. Each of them will know how many troops the other has, and none of them is fool enough to fight a stronger army than his own. So why would there be fighting? As I said, it's not the Brazilian way. The military will speak with one another by phone, but the president's phone won't be on. Not a word about this to anyone, you understand?" he added. "Not a word."

Carter wondered why Roberto had told them his plan at all. Perhaps to show the United States it was not needed. Or maybe he was already thinking about the possibility of USAID financing for the modernization of the telephone system after the coup. How much did his spooks know about all this, he wondered. He doubted they would let him know.

CHAPTER 7

Harry Martoni, CIA station chief in Brazil, was not happy. He picked up the memorandum on his desk and read it through again. "Son of a bitch," he said.

The memo was from the USAID legal advisor to the ambassador, and was classified "Secret." "Mr. Ambassador:" it read:

It has come to the attention of USAID/Legal that three cases of electric cattle prods consigned to USAID/AgDiv are being held by Brazilian customs awaiting submission of required documentation by USAID. These devices are used on farms to herd cattle and pigs from their paddocks into trucks, and again from trucks into and through slaughterhouses, as well as for other agricultural purposes. However, similar instruments have also been furnished by the CIA to several African and South American countries and allegedly used for the torture of political prisoners.

There appear to be at least two irregularities regarding this procurement.

First, there is no record of how this procurement was funded. There is no PIOP on file, nor has Legal been able to uncover any other legal source or authorization for funding by USAID.

Second, and perhaps more importantly, there is no existing USAID or USAID-funded agricultural project or program in which these devices might be legitimately employed. Indeed, the chief of AgDiv asserts that it did not order these devices, and has no knowledge of who ordered them, nor of their intended use.

As you are aware, pursuant to the provisions of the Foreign Assistance Act, USAID funds may only be used for development purposes. Use for political purposes is expressly forbidden. Moreover, the Antideficiency Act prohibits any use of funds by the US government except pursuant to written authorization. As noted above, Legal has been unable to find any written authorization for this procurement or its funding. Unless such documentation exists within the embassy, the acquisition appears to be unlawful.

Legal recommends that the items in question be left in Brazilian customs pending a detailed investigation regarding the possible irregularity of this procurement, and the intended use of the items purchased.

The document was signed "Peter J. Thornton, legal advisor, USAID." Across the bottom of the page was scrawled the word "concur," followed by Carter's signature and the acronym "AMB." It had been forwarded to the Embassy Investigations Office. A friend of Harry's there had sent a copy to him.

"Son of a bitch," Harry said again. There were several things about the memo that bothered him. Of course, he regretted the loss of the prods. He had promised them to General Oscar Cavalcanti, Chief of DOPS, the federal intelligence service of the Brazilian government. It was going to be embarrassing to tell him that he couldn't deliver. But what really bothered him was that somehow Thornton had found out about the prods, and what they were for. That phrase, "it has come to the attention of USAID Legal" was a dead giveaway. Obviously someone had told him, but who? Was the cover of his guy in the AgDiv blown? And why hadn't Carter consulted him before he approved Thornton's memo? He had worried for some time that Carter was talking with the Agency above his head, in Langley or perhaps in Rio, and without his knowledge. Maybe he knew more about what Harry was up to than he let on. He looked out the window at the never-ending rain. "Son of a bitch," he said for a third time.

Most CIA operatives in Rio were located on the eighth floor of the embassy building on Avenida Presidente Wilson. Their cover was the "political section" of the embassy. But there were two "political sections"—one on the fifth floor staffed by foreign service types, the other on the eighth floor manned by the spooks. All you had to do was ask a guy's room number, and you knew right away whether he worked for State or for the CIA.

Harry had turned down an office in the embassy building. His office was located on the sixth floor of a rather grubby office building on the Maua Square. Actually, all the buildings on the square were grubby. "Mow Square," as the sailors called it, adjoined the port section of Rio de Janeiro. Virtually every building contained at least one pick-up bar. They ran from elegant to sleazy. So did the whores. This suited Harry just fine. If you wanted a drink, you rode the ancient elevator down six floors to the Devil's Pleasure, on the ground floor. If you wanted sex, you picked up a piece, girl or boy, as you chose, and took her or him across the street to the Hotel Bleqaute. It took him a year before he figured out that *"Bleqaute"* meant "Blackout." It was all one helluva lot better than sitting in the embassy building on Avenida Presidente Wilson.

But the biggest advantage for a spook was that the headquarters of the military police was right across the square, and the War Ministry was only about three blocks away. Here at his office on the Praça Maua, he and the Brazilians could work together in privacy. No one saw or cared who came and went. No one had any idea who he was or why he was there.

The "why" was, of course, the coming coup, or the "Revolution to Restore Democracy," as it was called by the striped-pants set. Harry had never been able to figure why a military coup to throw out an elected civilian government should be called the "Revolution to Restore Democracy." But no matter what it was called, he had no doubt that Goulart's commie government had to go. And it was his job to make sure that happened.

Harry had spent the last two years cultivating the Brazilian military, providing them with small and large "gifts," running from surplus watering cans to scotch whiskey to Thompson machine guns. And it had paid off. He was on a first-name basis with most of the generals and the colonels, certainly the important ones. They had drunk together, overeaten together, gone whoring together. Not bad work for a spy. And so they had let him in on what was happening, not because they didn't know who he was, but because they did. They knew where the butter on their bread came from.

Looking out the window he could see General Oscar Cavalcanti in jeans and a rain jacket maneuvering his way around the puddles in the Praça Maua. A few minutes later he was in Harry's office.

"What shitty weather," the general said, taking off his jacket and shaking the water onto the rug. "And this is supposed to be summer."

"Want to go downstairs for a drink? It'll warm you up."

The general shook his head no.

"I've got a little Johnnie Walker right here. How about a snort, just to warm up with?"

"Sure," said the general. "No harm in that."

Harry poured him a double of Red Label. The general gulped it down. "That's the real stuff," he said appreciatively. "Nothing fake in that."

"Not for you," said Harry.

The general smiled. "That's what I like about your outfit," he said. "You may be spies, but you never try to fool your friends. But your embassy. . . . " His voice trailed away. Then he brightened again, "We've picked up a few of the kids who've been making some noise for Goulart. I'm sure they know what's going on, but I can't lay a hand on them. Their parents are all those upper-class elite types who live along the beach out in Ipanema or Leblon. If some of their kids get hurt, and if the revolution fails, we could have a real problem on our hands. . . . You've got those electric prods for me, don't you?"

Harry had seen it coming, but there was nothing much he could do. "I'm sorry, Oscar. The shipment's been held up. Seems the manufacturer ran short. This is pork-slaughtering time in Nebraska, and they sold out of prods. We couldn't find any anywhere. The manufacturer is working overtime to fill our order. It may be a couple of weeks. I'm sorry."

Cavalcanti scowled. "Bullshit, Harry. I just got through saying you guys don't try to fool us, and here you are handing me a line of pure bullshit. You teach us how to use them, then you can't get 'em for us because it's pig-slaughtering time in Nebraska? Don't fuck with me, Harry. You know I can close down your whole fucking operation here in two minutes if I want to. You tell me what happened, and tell it to me straight."

Harry looked at the General, who suddenly seemed to resemble an enraged pit bull. "OK," he said. "I'm sorry, but I can't get them for you. The ambassador found out. He's ordered them held in customs until he can find out why they were shipped, and to whom. There's nothing I can do."

The General exploded. "Well, fuck him. Customs is part of the Brazilian government, not the US. That goddamn striped-pants fairy can't order them held in our customs. I'm going to order them released." He reached for Harry's phone. "Right now," he said.

"I wouldn't do that, Oscar. I agree he's a pain in the ass, but he *is* the ambassador of the United States of America. You don't want to piss him off with C-Day coming up. They do listen to him in Washington. And incidentally, he's not a fairy. He's got a wife. And one of our guys spotted him talking with a chickie at a bar in Copa a week ago. We haven't got hard proof yet. But we're working on it."

Cavalcanti sat down again. "Shit," he said. Harry decided to say nothing.

"Is he against the revolution?"

"He can't be against the coup officially. It's the 'policy' of the United States to support it, to make it happen. We've given a few million dollars to a few governors who are supporting your side. But if it were up to him, we'd be standing aside just waiting to see what happens. He seems to believe all that crap about supporting 'democratically elected governments,' and about the rule of international law." Harry fiddled with the mustache on his upper lip. "Oh, I like the sound of that stuff as well as the next guy, but it's not realistic. And it won't protect my country from the commies."

The general was lost in thought. Finally, he looked up at Harry. "The United States wouldn't like it if the ambassador disappeared, would it?"

Harry was puzzled. "Of course not," he said.

"And if it appeared that he had been kidnapped by a cell of young Communist supporters of Jango, and Jango did nothing about it, that would be a pretty good reason for a military coup against Goulart, wouldn't it?"

Harry looked at the general in disbelief. "And where in the hell would the army find a bunch of leftist kids to kidnap the American ambassador?"

Cavalcanti smiled. "For a spook, you're not that quick, are you? Of course, they're not leftist kids, Harry, they are soldiers making believe they are leftist kids, soldiers who would love to be promoted to sergeant, earn a medal, and maybe draw thirty days TDI on a nice beach somewhere in the Northeast. Of course, if any of them even breathe a word about what really happened, we shoot him."

"You're serious, aren't you?"

The general nodded.

"And what happens to Carter?"

"Oh, we hold him in a basement somewhere in Santa Teresa or maybe Tijuca for a few days, and then our soldiers 'rescue' him from the 'commie kids' once the coup is over and he can't do any harm." Cavalcanti gazed at Harry through half-closed eyes. "Of course, we'd need a little information from your team. Like what time he goes to and from work, what's his normal route, what car he drives, who's his driver, whatever you can find out about his girlfriend, if he has one— like where she lives—that kind of stuff. We'll take care of the rest."

Harry drew in a large breath. The Agency help the Brazilian Army kidnap the United States ambassador? As far as he knew, it had never done *that* before. "I don't think we can do that, Oscar," he said.

The general got up from his chair. "I don't think you *can't* do it, Harry," he said, "if you want your guys to go on operating here." He picked up his jacket and walked out of the door.

It was a good Brazilian lunch: rice, garlicky black beans, fried potatoes, *farofa*, a well-done fillet steak that weighed at least half a kilo, four glasses of *chopp*, a *cafezinho*, and a good Bahian cigar. Pity, Cavalcanti thought, to go back to work. A nap would be much nicer. But this work was actually going to be a pleasure. The cattle prods would have been more satisfying, but this project wasn't bad either. He picked up the phone and waited. Four minutes later he had a dial tone. He dialed hastily lest the line drop before he got through.

Colonel Augusto Bastos de Melo, chief of staff for the Third Division of the Second Army stationed in Rio, answered the phone himself. *"Alo,"* he shouted into the phone, *"Quem fala?"*

"It's me," Cavalcanti replied. "Oscar."

"Oscar, what Oscar?"

"Oscar Cavalcanti," he shouted back. If Augusto could destroy his eardrums, he could destroy Augusto's.

"Oh, why didn't you say so?"

"I did."

"What?" Colonel de Melo shouted.

Oscar decided to leave the introductory conversation there. "Listen Augusto, I need your help."

"What?"

"I need your help. I need ten or twelve young recruits maybe seventeen or eighteen years old for about two weeks, and I want them before you guys chop their hair off. Long-haired students would be best. You know, kids."

There was silence on the line.

"Shit," Cavalcanti said out loud. "The goddamn line's dropped!"

"No, it hasn't dropped," de Melo said. "Have you gone queer on me or something?"

Cavalcanti laughed. "No, Augusto," he said. "I've not gone queer. I need about a dozen recruits to play college students in a little project we are setting up."

"Oh," de Melo said. "Well, that's all right, I guess. Sure, I can get them for you. When do you need them?"

"Tomorrow," Cavalcanti said. "Or Friday. We are going to have to train them. And Augusto, could you send half a dozen pistols along with them? Any big model will do. We want them to be seen."

"Sure," Colonel de Melo said.

"And one more thing. Would you have a couple of old cars you can lend us? Not military vehicles, some old sedans."

"That's harder," de Melo said. "I don't have any of those. I suppose we could steal you some," he said doubtfully. "A couple of old taxis maybe."

"No," Oscar said. "Never mind. I'll find some."

CHAPTER 8

For over a week Carter had wrestled with his conscience. Like Jack Sprague said, he was a married man. He had never cheated on Priscilla before. And he was the ambassador of the United States of America. If he were caught with a whore he would be fired. Not that you could call her a whore. Maybe a call girl, or perhaps a streetwalker. But never a whore. Not with that sparkle in her eye. Not with her little factory in Bangu where she made clothes for tots. Not working for another ambassador, passing out books at a diplomatic reception, even if she was sleeping with him on the side. Almost any ambassador in Brazil would sleep with a girl like that. But the *American* ambassador? Not if he wanted to keep his job. And his wife.

Still, he thought, he might drive out to Posto 6 sometime and have another drink at the Bar Atlantico. That wouldn't do any harm. Marina probably wouldn't be there anyway. And if she were there, they'd just have a drink together. Like friends, nothing more. But he felt excitement in his stomach. It'll go away, he thought, though he sort of hoped it wouldn't.

There was little Carter liked less about his job than hosting visiting dignitaries. Like the governor of the state of Nebraska, who was, at that moment, regaling him about his own importance at the restaurant of the Ouro Verde Hotel. The hotel was on the Avenida Atlantica, near the opposite end of Copacabana Beach from the Bar Atlantico, but he could see its red neon sign flickering in the distance. Priscilla was in Sao Paulo presiding over the annual meeting of the Brazil-American Literary Society. Maybe this would be a good night to stop by the bar just for a nightcap after he got rid of the governor.

The dinner dragged on until midnight, and it wasn't until 12:30 a.m. that Carter arrived at the bar. He found a seat near the back and ordered a caipirinha. It's too late, he said to himself. By now she was sure to be in bed, with one of her johns, or without one.

"Welcome back, Mr. Ambassador," Marina said from behind him. "I've missed you. Are you taking a little night air?"

He could feel his breathing speeding up already. "Hello Marina." He tried to sound casual. "What a coincidence that we meet again."

Marina walked around to the front of the table and sat down next to him. She wore a tight pair of low-waisted jeans, a wide leather belt, a navy blue low-cut blouse, and platform shoes. She was not wearing a brassiere, and he could see the shape of her breasts and her dark nipples through her blouse.

"Don't stare, Tony," she said. "It's not polite."

"I'm sorry," he said. "It's just that . . . well, you are very pretty." His attempt at sounding casual totally failed. "How's the factory?" he asked.

Marina ignored the question. "You're not bad looking yourself," she said. She ran her fingers through his hair. "Buy me a caipirinha?"

"Sure," he said.

The waiter came over. "Another caipirinha," Carter said. The waiter went away.

"Can I drink some of yours until mine comes?" she asked.

"Sure," he said again. He watched her put his glass to her lips and take a small sip. A smudge of her scarlet lipstick stayed on the glass. She passed it back to him, the lipstick on his side.

"Thanks," she said.

Carter took the next sip. The sweet taste of her lipstick blended in his mouth with the lemon-sour of the drink.

"Did you know it would taste like that?" he asked.

"Yes," she said. "But it's even better without the caipirinha." She leaned over next to him, resting her hand gently on his thigh. He could see down her blouse. "Want a taste?" she asked, her hand moving up his thigh.

Carter moved her hand away. "No," he meant to say. But his lips were now covered by hers, and her tongue was moving into his mouth.

Marina drew her lips away. "Let's go," she said.

One kiss, Carter thought, and he had already gotten hard. His heart was racing. "Alright," he stammered.

He paid the bill and the two of them strolled along the beach toward Rua Siqueira Campos. It was after 1 a.m. and the traffic on the Avenue had died away. The waves crashing ashore left little pools and streams in the sand. Suddenly Marina scooped off her platform sandals and raced out toward the water.

"Come on," she shouted to him. He struggled to take off his wing tips and black socks, then followed her down to the water's edge. The water washed warm over his toes. Then her feet were between his, and her breasts were pressed up against his chest. Another wave came ashore and soaked them both to their knees.

Marina pulled her body away from his and unbuttoned her blouse.

"Last time *I* kissed *you*. Now it's your turn," she said.

God, he thought, maybe she's a streetwalker, but she's walking with me. He put his arms around her and pulled her toward him. He could feel her arms moving up around his neck. He kissed her, long and hard.

"Let's go to my house," Marina said, when he finally pulled away. "Maybe we'll play house . . . or maybe school. Maybe you can learn a thing or two."

School was fantastic, like nothing he had ever done before.

Marina taught him things Priscilla would not even dream of doing. She actually got him to come three times, twice in her vagina, once between her lips, each time better than the last. Finally, near five in the morning, Marina looked at him all over and gave his penis a French kiss. "School's over." She said. "You're a good student. You get an A."

"That was amazing," Carter said.

He reached for his trousers and took out a $100 bill. "That's not tuition," he said. "It's an investment in the factory."

Marina smiled. "You're a sweet man," she said.

CHAPTER 9

For a change, Carter thought, the spooks and the real political section had reached the same conclusion: A coup was coming. Or better said, one of two coups. He expertly maneuvered the Fusca around two gigantic potholes.

"On the one hand," a memo the political section sent him yesterday read,

> Goulart is considering his own coup that would strengthen his position by suspending the constitution, firing a number of cabinet members and military officers of doubtful loyalty to him, and closing the congress. The idea is for him to run the country by fiat for the next sixty days. What would happen after that hasn't been decided.

"On the other hand," the memo continued,

> a large number of generals and other military officers are persuaded that Jango has to go. Although he was democratically and legally elected, they believe he has now "subverted the democratic process" by turning sharply to the left, contrary to the will of the Brazilian people. They believe that he is now showing his true Communist colors, and that a military coup is necessary to restore democracy to Brazil.

Incredibly, Carter thought, a significant number of the foreign service officers at the embassy, and virtually the entire Brazil Desk at State, actually believed this "restore democracy" crap. Since when could a military coup against a democratically elected government "restore democracy"? Worse, Washington seemed to believe that the United States had a "duty to the hemisphere" to support the Brazilian military's plans. He swerved to the right to avoid a bus that seemed to be intent on crushing his VW between itself and the truck on the other side of him. "What bullshit," he said out loud.

In any event, to be safe, he had two weeks ago directed the admin section to notify all persons on the embassy's register of American citizens living in Brazil that there was a serious risk of possible unrest, and if any movement of military units should occur, they should stay at home and not go out into the streets. With some trepidation, he had also directed his military attaché, General Otto Werner, to ask the navy to make a troop transport vessel available in Guanabara Bay in case it became necessary to evacuate American tourists or residents.

"Good morning, Mr. Ambassador," Joannie smiled at him from behind her desk when he arrived at the embassy. She always smiled, Carter thought. And she got for him whatever he needed, whenever he needed it.

"Anything new?" he asked.

"There's a bunch of stuff on your desk; garbage mostly, and then there's this."

She handed him a large envelope stamped "Top Secret." It was red. That meant it came from the secretary of state, and that meant that the top echelons were once again sticking their noses into things they knew little about. "Shit," he said.

"Oh, come on." Joannie said. "You haven't even opened it yet. Maybe it's an invitation to a fancy dress ball at the White House."

He grunted.

"I've got some good news, too. General Werner is waiting to see you." Werner was one of the few people at the embassy Carter knew he could trust. He was always glad to see him.

"Tell General Werner I'll be with him in a few moments," Carter said.

As he thought, the cable in the red envelope was from the secretary of state.

Dear Anthony:

We have carefully reviewed your cable dated March 18 relating to the rally on March 16 in Rio. The speeches of Governor Brizola and President Goulart provide grounds for particular concern, as do the hammer and sickle flags in the crowd. These events, together with the government's failure to respond vigorously to the Sailors' Revolt leads us to the conclusion that we cannot stand idly by while Brazil, and potentially the whole of Latin America, slips under Communist control.

I am informed by the Brazil Desk that you have direct access to President Goulart, and that your relationship is cordial. You are instructed to seek an immediate personal appointment with President Goulart on an individual and confidential basis. You are to inform him that we cannot continue to countenance the present situation. In accordance with Atlantic Convention, the Monroe Doctrine, and the Alliance for Progress, we demand that he sever all ties with Luiz Carlos Prestes and the Brazilian labor movement, and dismiss from his government all of the persons on the attached list by no later than 2400 hours on March 31, failing which we shall consider ourselves free to take such action as may be necessary and appropriate to protect Brazil and the hemisphere from Communist control, and to restore Brazil to democratic rule. You may assure the president that if he complies with our request, we will see to it that he is protected against any risk to his person or to his family that might otherwise arise.

—Regards, Rusk

Attached to the secretary's cable was a list that included virtually all of Jango's cabinet.

Carter drew a deep breath. He wasn't surprised by most of the secretary's cable. He had expected something like this. But the last sentence was chilling. He read it again. "You may assure the president that if he complies with our request, we will see to it that he is protected against any risk to his person or to his family that might otherwise arise." And if he does not comply? Carter thought. Does the cable mean that if he does not bend to our will, he will be "removed," as the spooks so delicately put it? There was no chance that Goulart would comply. Still, he had no choice but to present the secretary's ultimatum to Goulart. He was the American ambassador. Those were his instructions.

Carter put the cable back in the red envelope, put it in the top drawer of his desk, and buzzed Joannie on the intercom. "Show in General Werner, please," he said.

Brigadier General Otto Werner was a large man. He held his back ramrod straight, so that his six-foot-two body looked as if he were six foot four. On his barrel chest were something like twenty ribbons representing everything from two Purple Hearts to the Patton Medal of Honor on the field of battle. He had a proper military brush haircut, a perfectly pressed air force uniform, and, of course, spit-polished shoes. He was walking now into Carter's office with a slight limp, the result of a crash landing of his B-47 during the Korean war.

"Good morning, Mr. Ambassador," he said, as he gave Carter a bone-crushing handshake. "You think it'll ever stop raining?"

"Not too soon," Carter said. "It's just like Elis Regina sings it: *'Chove chuva, chove sem parar.'* Not bad in English either: It's raining rain, endless rain. . . . But it can't rain on this poor country forever. It'll stop one day."

"Se Deus quiser," said the general. If God wishes it.

The weather out of the way, it was time to talk business. "So what are your soldier friends up to?" Carter said.

Werner was bilingual in Portuguese and English. He also spoke fluent German, French, Italian, Spanish, Turkish, Russian, and Greek. After many years as language interpreter for the White House, he had spent almost two decades teaching tactics of guerilla warfare at the National War College to military officers from America's allies around the world. He believed he should speak their languages if his lessons were to be understood. But he thought his charges should learn English in return.

His first group of students had been from Brazil, billeted at Andrews Air Force Base just outside Washington. Although he spoke not a word of Portuguese, Werner moved in with them. Mornings they all spoke Portuguese, afternoons and evenings they spoke English. After dinner at the base, they headed out to the bars in Alexandria or on Capitol Hill, or occasionally to one of the pick-up joints on Fourteenth Street. Within a few weeks, they were communicating pretty well.

The Brazilians were puzzled, though. Colonel Azevedo Leitao, one of the younger colonels, asked him one night at a bar in Arlington, "Where do your people go to fuck? We have our motels outside Rio where you can rent a room for four hours at a time for just a few cruzeiros. But I went to one of your motels in Arlington with a really cute girl the other night, and they would only let me have a room for the whole night, and they charged just like the Hilton. I couldn't afford it. And I had to pay the girl anyway."

It was a good question, Werner thought, especially if you were a foreigner in Washington for just a few months. He took the keys out of his pocket. "I have a little apartment in Georgetown," he told Azevedo.

Next time you need it, just let me know. But I'll charge you to get the sheets washed," he added. They both laughed. "Have another beer," said Colonel Azevedo happily. "On me."

And now, some twenty years later, General Azevedo was chief of the Fourth Army stationed in Salvador, Bahia. In fact, most of the generals who were conspiring to bring down Goulart had been Werner's drinking buddies back then: Braga, Costa, Leitao, Medici, Cavalcanti, and many others. And no small number of them had enjoyed their American sex lives in his apartment in Georgetown. Slowly, but surely, his friends had made it up the military ladder to the rank of general. He had kept in touch and remained friends with his old buddies to the present day. Marshal Braga was at the top of the heap.

"So what's up?" Carter said again. "What are your friends telling you?"

"Not much," said Werner. "They're holding their cards pretty close to the chest. As far as I can see, Braga is the one in charge, although Leitao thinks he is. At least he wants to be. There's no doubt that they intend to force Jango out. The question is when. Of course, Jango may try to pull off his own coup first. He's got some support in the military too."

"Any idea of a possible date?"

"Not yet . . . possibly early April, but there's no way of saying."

"Any risk to Jango's life?"

"Not really. Not on their side, although General Cavalcanti would like to do it. '*Segurança*' he calls it: 'Security.' But as far as I can tell, the rest are prepared to let Jango and Brizola skip out to Uruguay. Brizola is Jango's brother-in-law. As you know, he's the governor of the State of Rio Grande do Sul, a Communist and a fanatic for the cause."

Werner paused for a moment. "I'm not sure what our spooks have in mind. Not my department. Harry Martoni and Cavalcanti are pretty good buddies. They must know. But you must know about all that."

I wish I did, Carter thought. Ever since Harry had moved to the

Praça Maua, Carter had little idea what he was doing. Martoni made little effort to keep him informed. Since the CIA had its own cable equipment, Carter could not even monitor their cable traffic. They knew more than he did.

"How about the troop carrier? Have we got an ETA?" he asked.

"Well," Werner said, "the ships have left the Caribbean. . . . "

"What do you mean 'ships'? It's one ship, one troop carrier, that's all."

"That's right," Werner said. "One ship."

"You said 'ships.' That means more than one."

Werner took a deep breath. "I'm sorry, Mr. Ambassador. There is more than one. I thought you knew that."

Carter glared at his military attaché. "How many?"

Werner fiddled with one of the ribbons on his chest.

"How many, goddamn it?"

Werner was looking at his shoes. Carter could see his left knee, the one made of nickel, begin to tremble. "Twelve," Werner said. "Four tankers, six destroyers, and the troop carrier."

"That's only eleven," Carter snapped.

There was a long silence. "And an aircraft carrier," Werner said. There was another silence. "They're supposed to steam into Guanabara Bay when they get here, to show support for the generals. The whole operation is called Brother Sam. It's absolutely top secret."

"Son of a bitch!" With each word, Carter slammed his fist down on his desk.

Werner's knee was trembling more violently now. "Don't shoot the messenger," he said.

"I don't mean you. I mean Washington. Why in hell didn't they let me know? I'm supposed to be the head of the country team. . . . Actually, why in hell didn't *you* let me know?"

"Because I didn't know either," Werner said. "Admiral Whitcroft only called me last night. That's why I asked Joannie if I could see you this morning."

"When will they get here?"

"I don't know. Maybe by the end of the month. Maybe April 1 or 2. Whitcroft wouldn't say."

"Do the generals know they're coming?"

"I spoke with a couple of them last night," Werner said. "They didn't seem to. I haven't spoken yet with Marshal Braga."

"They haven't asked for our help?"

"No sir, not that I know of."

There was a pause. "We've got to turn those ships around," Carter said. "If they steam into Guanabara Bay, it'll screw up our relationship with Brazil for years to come, whether the coup succeeds or not. It'll destroy everything Kennedy did for our image in Latin America before he was killed. It will end the Alliance for Progress. Neither Jango *nor* the military will put up with our screwing around in Brazil's internal affairs this way. Actually, it's the only thing that could drive Jango and the generals into each others' arms against us. This time the Desk has gone completely out of their minds."

Werner looked out the window at the Sugarloaf through the rain. "I know," he said quietly. "But they couldn't be doing this without the president. It's too big."

"If that's true, he's gone crazy as well," Carter said.

Werner left Carter's office with a visible limp. It was the first time, Carter realized, that he had seen his perennially optimistic military attaché looking worried. With good reason, Carter thought.

How could Otto know about the flotilla when he, the ambassador, didn't? They hadn't told him one word about it, much less asked his advice. That couldn't be accidental. You don't just "forget" to tell the ambassador. Obviously, they didn't want him to know. Were they trying to work with the generals behind his back? But who were "they"? State? The Agency?

A twin engine Varig Electra was taking off from Santos Dumont Airport across from the embassy. He watched it swing to the left to avoid Sugarloaf, then straighten course as it passed to the right of the naval fort in the middle of the bay before heading out to sea.

Planes, he thought. Nobody sends an aircraft carrier without planes: combat planes, hidden below the decks of the carrier, to provide air cover to the Brazilian military if they needed it, if the fighting turned nasty. They would be available to bomb the presidential palace in Laranjeiras, as well as any of the Brazilian armies that supported Goulart. There was no risk to the American planes: There were no anti-aircraft batteries in Brazil and the Brazilian Air Force was a joke. Basically, the United States was preparing to invade, but they hadn't told him. If Otto hadn't slipped up, he wouldn't know now.

Carter walked back to his desk. He waited a minute to calm down, then picked up the red secure phone and dialed Otto's number. "I'm sorry, Mr. Ambassador, he isn't back yet," the general's secretary said. Just as well, Carter thought. He waited another minute before he flicked on the intercom again.

"Joannie, I'm going to need an appointment with the president."

"Which one?" she said, smiling.

Ordinarily Carter would have laughed, but not now. "You know which one," he snapped.

"I'm sorry, chief," Joannie said. "For when?"

Carter looked at his watch. It was four thirty already. "Tomorrow," he said, "as early as you can get it." He picked up the secretary of state's cable and read it through one more time. The closing sentence sent a shudder down his spine, just as it had when he first read it.

"You may assure the president that if he complies with our request, we will see to it that he is protected against any risk to his person or his family which might otherwise arise."

Did the cable mean that if Goulart did not comply, neither the president nor his family would be free of risk? He knew what sort of risk, and it horrified him.

Carefully, Carter folded the cable up, put it back in the red envelope and put the envelope into the safe under the picture of Lyndon Johnson on the wall behind his desk. "You're fucking up big time this time around, Mr. President." he said to the picture. "Big time."

CHAPTER 10

He deserved a drink. No doubt about it, he deserved a drink. And some company. There was no point in going to the residence. Priscilla was in Sao Paolo attending a meeting of the Garden Club. Even if she has been in Rio, she would not be speaking with him. Things weren't going so well between them. He needed a caipirinha.

Carter rode his elevator down to the basement. "I'm taking the Fusca," he said to Joaozinho. "You can go home."

There were still a few couples on the terrace at the Bar Atlantico when he arrived.

"Hello, Mr. Fulano," Guilherme said. "The usual?"

Carter nodded.

Fulano meant "anybody." So, in the Bar Atlantico, he was Mr. Anybody, exactly who he wanted to be. Anybody but the American ambassador.

Guilherme was back with his drink a few moments later. "Your friend was here," he said. "She was looking for you."

Carter sat fiddling with his drink. What does she want, he wondered. Was it the money? Or was there something more? And what did *he* want? The sex was spectacular, but was he looking for something more?

He felt her fingers on the back of his neck.

"Hi," Marina said.

"Hi."

He turned to look at her. Instead of her fishnet stockings and streetwalker clothes, she was wearing a pair of corduroy pants, sandals, and a gray sweater. As usual, there was no brassiere. She wore almost no makeup.

"What's this," he said, "a day off from the street?"

Marina looked hurt. "I thought you'd like it if I dressed up like an American woman," she said. "So you'd feel more at home."

"You don't look like an American woman," Carter said. "You're much too beautiful."

Marina smiled. "You're sweet," she said. "Do you want to go fuck?"

"Sure," he said. But it was so unromantic. "Let's go somewhere first."

"OK," she said, "Where do you want to go?"

"I don't know."

Marina looked up at the sky. "It's a good moon," she said. "Do you have your car here?"

"Sure," he said again.

"Would you let me drive it?"

"Do you know how to drive a Fusca?"

Marina laughed. "Do you know Hans Klaus? He's the president of Volkswagen do Brasil?"

Carter nodded.

"His name is on one of my sewing machines. Any more questions?" She paused. "Have you been to Sao Conrado?" she asked. "I think you'll like it."

Marina drove expertly through the streets at the end of Copacabana to the road which skirted the beach at Ipanema and Leblon. Two gigantic red-gray rocks, each perhaps 500 feet high, towered over the far end of the beach. "Those are Dois Irmaos," Marina said. "Two Brothers. Aren't they beautiful?"

"What are those little lights sparkling around the base of it?"

"Oh, that's the Vidigal favela. They have some of the most fabulous views in the world. They pay next to nothing for the view, but the apartments along the beach here in Ipanema cost a fortune." She was sailing through a red light at ninety kilometers an hour.

"Hey," Carter exclaimed. "That was a red light!"

Marina smiled. "This is Rio de Janeiro, Tony," she said. "We don't care much about red lights after ten o'clock at night. You could get held up."

The paving stopped at the end of Leblon. On the left, a dirt road continued on along the bottom of Dois Irmaos. Marina headed for it. "This is going to be the main road to Sao Conrado some day, if they ever finish it." The car skidded suddenly toward the ocean. "Hold on, it's a bit slippery," she said.

The road was cut into the side of the rock, some fifty feet above the ocean. The left side of the road was on a veritable cliff. Carter closed his eyes.

Somehow, Marina kept the VW on the road. "Look," she shouted above the sound of the waves a few minutes up the road after they had left the pavement. A small modern motel stood by the side of the road. "Some of us go there to fuck sometimes, but it's expensive." The car dropped into a puddle and skidded halfway across the road. "Do you want to stop there?"

"Yes," Carter replied.

"Neither do I," Marina said.

Ten minutes later the road swerved to the right and dropped down to the beach. Except for the side toward the ocean, the beach was completely surrounded by a tropical rain forest and the mountains. He could see several islands near the dark horizon between sky and sea, with what he thought must be the tops of palm trees, although they were too far away for him to tell.

Dois Irmaos stood directly behind them. At the other end of the beach stood another huge red-gray rock, which seemed to have been chopped off at the top by a giant stone cutter a thousand centuries ago.

"That's the Pedra da Gavea," Marina said. "Gavea Rock. Isn't it wonderful?"

The beach was empty except for a small white church up against the forest and an even smaller wooden building near the end of the beach. A sign on the building read "Bar" and underneath it, a second read *"Peixe Frito,"* fried fish. A third sign read "Closed."

Marina pulled the car off the road, took off her sandals and got out.

"What do you think, Mr. Ambassador? This is Sao Conrado and for tonight it's all yours." She took off her sweater and dropped it on the sand. "And so am I." She set off toward Dos Irmaos on the wet sand near the water. "Bet you can't catch me," she shouted.

"That's a bet," Carter shouted back.

He lost. Marina reached the end of the beach long before he did.

"No fair," he said, as he panted his way up to her. He looked down at her breasts. "No fair," he said again. "I was distracted."

"I've told you before," Marina said. "Don't stare. It's not polite."

A few feet beyond them, Carter saw a bottle standing upright in the sand, together with a bunch of wilted flowers and a candle blown out by the wind.

"That's a small temple made by someone for Yemanja," Marina said. "She's the goddess of the sea. We leave gifts for her: flowers, cachaca, and sometimes some jewelry. The candle is so she can see her way to shore. She swims in close every New Year's Eve. She's very important."

"Does she have a fish tail?" Carter asked.

Marina looked at him. "How did you know?" she asked.

"Just guessing," Carter said.

They walked slowly back down the beach, splashing now and again through the shallow pools left by the tide. Marina stopped and opened the button at her waist. Her slacks and panties fell to the sand.

"Let's go in," she said. She stepped backwards into the pool. "Come on in," she said again, "the water's fine. And warm."

It was only about a foot deep. Carter slowly took off his shirt, pants, and underwear and slipped nude into the water. Marina was lying on her back, looking at the sky.

"Look at the moon," she said.

Carter moved over to her and gently spread her legs apart.

"Make believe you love me," Marina whispered.

That wasn't going to be hard, he thought.

CHAPTER 11

"**W**hy do American women insist on making themselves unhappy?" General Jorge Augusto Moura had asked him at a dinner party in his home soon after Carter arrived in Brazil some two years ago. Moura was a large and jovial *general reformado*, which, Carter had learned, meant retired, not reformed. The general had been attaché at the Brazilian embassy in Washington for many years. He was now spending his retirement at USAID, working half time as advisor to Brazil's national security program, i.e., the cops. Carter liked him nevertheless.

"What do you mean, General?" Carter asked.

"Well, look at it this way. Suppose you and I were each having an affair. I'm sure you're not, but just suppose. In the United States, your American wife would break her neck to find out whether you were having an affair, and if so, with whom. If and when she did find out, there would be a tremendous fight between the two of you, very likely you split up, and she is miserable. Ten years later she realizes that actually you and she were pretty good together, but it's too late. You have moved in with your mistress, and your ex-wife is old and ugly and will never catch another man.

"Now a Brazilian wife knows that knowing about her husband's peccadilloes will bring her nothing but grief. In fact, she goes to great lengths *not* to find out. For instance, look right here in this room."

He waved his hand toward his guests who were chatting with one another after dinner, the women clustered at one end of the room, the men at the other. "The men are talking about soccer, a bit of politics, and their mistresses," he said. "You see how the women are sitting at the other end of the room, as far away as they can get from their husbands? They are talking nonstop about their children and their maids—*cri cri*, we call it—to be certain that they do *not* hear what their husbands are saying about their lovers or about where they fuck them. So long as the wives don't know, there's nothing they need to do about it. Their lives go on, well off, reasonably good sex with their husbands from time to time and contented. And some of them may even be the mistresses of the men to whom their husbands are talking at the other end of the room."

It was all so different than at home. So very different. "But what about love?" Carter said.

"Love?" Moura said, "There's love, and there's sex. Sometimes they go together, and sometimes they don't. They are so different: Love is love. Sex is sex. Surely a man can love one woman—his wife, for example—and go to bed with another one. That's the way it is in Brazil. That's the way it is in the United States as well, but you make believe it isn't.

"And let me tell you something else. Sex with another woman can save a marriage. Suppose my wife and I are truly in love, but the sex is terrible. If I can get a little good sex somewhere else from time to time, my marriage is still OK, even though we don't have good sex together. But if I don't get a little on the outside, our love will turn sour, and our marriage will as well. . . . "

"Is all that really true?"

"Oh, maybe not among the youngsters. It's hard to buy if you're a nineteen-year-old beauty, and love is new. But wait until she's thirty or forty. She knows by then that love and sex may go together, but not always. And if she isn't careful, she'll destroy the love, just because her man is getting a little sex on the side—and she knows about it."

"But what if *she's* getting some on the side?" Carter asked.

Moura had looked at him and sighed. "Sometimes you gringos just don't get it," he said. "Women are different. They don't need it like we do. You're new here, Mr. Ambassador. When in Brazil, do as the Brazilians do, and you'll be fine."

Joaozinho had turned the car onto Rua Sao Clemente, and they crawled along now through the traffic heading toward the residence. Out of habit, Carter glanced at the rearview mirror. Behind them was a black 1949 Plymouth sedan. He had seen that car before, he thought. In fact, it had been behind them as they drove down Botafogo Beach before turning onto Sao Clemente. He leaned forward and tapped on the glass that separated the front seat from the back. "Joaozinho," he said, "turn left on Rua Real Grandeza."

"Yes, sir."

Carter watched in the mirror as the black sedan turned behind them. "Head for the tunnel," he said to Joaozinho.

"Yes, sir."

They drove up Real Grandeza toward the Tunel Velho. On the other side of the tunnel was Copacabana. At the exit from the tunnel, Carter knew, the road split into Santa Clara on the left and Siqueira Campos—Marina's street—on the right. "When we get out of the tunnel, drive fast as if you're going down Siqueira Campos," he said. "Then, at the last minute, take Avenida Santa Clara."

Joaozinho did it beautifully. He sped down Rua Real Grandeza close to the center line, barreled through the tunnel, slowed down at the end, signaled a right turn, then just where the road split, he swung hard to the left, over the sidewalk, just missing a concrete telephone pole, and sped down Santa Clara. There was no way the black sedan could follow without hitting the pole. Carter could hear the sound of shattering glass behind them as the sedan crashed into it.

"Nicely done," Carter said. "Let's head for the residence again. But it doesn't need to be quite so exciting this time around."

What was that all about, he thought. He had been heading for the residence. Who would want to follow him there? It was no secret where he lived. Was someone planning a kidnapping? Why would anyone want to kidnap him? Or were they trying to frighten him? Well, they had succeeded in doing that.

Carter knew that Priscilla would follow General Moura's script for an American wife. And he knew that the General was also right that if she found out about Marina, their marriage would be over. She was in the right, of course. He had not been faithful to her. But, he thought, where was it written that you could only love one woman at a time? He certainly loved both his children, now fully grown. He could love both Rio de Janeiro and his weekend house in Vermont at the same time. He could love both his mother and his father equally. In fact, the question of who he loved more would never even come up. In many parts of the world, men had more than one wife. There was no reason why he could not love both Marina and Priscilla at the same time. But Priscilla believed none of it.

"Did you have a good meeting?" he said after a perfunctory kiss.

"The meeting ended early," she said. "I flew back here last night. Where were you?"

Well, this is it, Carter thought. It's been coming, and now it's here. But more out of habit than anything else, he said, "At the office."

"You know that's a lie."

"Why do you want to know? Will it help?"

"Because I am your wife, that's why. Where were you last night?"

"Will it make you any happier if you know?"

"It's not my happiness," Priscilla hissed. "I am your wife. I have a right to know."

Carter sighed. He was tired of the fights, of living a lie. "All right," he said. "I was with my Brazilian girlfriend. But that doesn't mean. . . . "

"You bastard," Priscilla said softly. "You miserable bastard."

Carter knew there was no point in talking about it. General Moura was right. Priscilla wouldn't listen, she certainly wouldn't understand.

"I'll bet she's a whore," she said.

"No," Carter said, "she's not." She once was, he thought, but she's not now. I love you both, he wanted to say, but Priscilla had already stormed out of the room, slamming the door behind her. It was good she didn't really know that Marina had been a streetwalker, he thought. That might cause her to simply snap.

He wound up sleeping in one of the residence's guest rooms, and arrived at the embassy in the morning at 8:30, an ungodly hour for him. As usual, Joannie was there ahead of him.

"You're early, Mr. Ambassador," she said. "Didn't you sleep well? And how's Mrs. Carter?"

Carter chose to ignore her questions. "Did you make that appointment with President Goulart?"

"Yes, sir," she said. "It wasn't easy. His appointment secretary is a real pill. But I finally got you in at eleven."

"11:00 a.m. or p.m.?" In Brazil you couldn't be sure.

She laughed. "a.m."

"Then I guess I'd better get ready. Get that cable from the secretary of state out of the safe for me, would you?"

He sat in his office and read the cable one more time. He couldn't simply give Goulart a copy. It was classified "Top Secret." Besides, it would make Jango apoplectic, and understandably so. No, he would have to soften it down, but without losing the message that Washington wanted him to convey.

CHAPTER 12

Carter's limousine, with the American flag flying from each front fender not withstanding the rain, turned off Rua das Laranjeiras and drove through Parque Guinle to the gate of the Laranjeiras Presidential Palace. The guard peered into the car and waved him through. Goulart's second secretary stood at the door to the visitor's entrance awaiting him. Usually it would have been the first secretary. It's going to be a tough visit, Carter thought as he followed the secretary up the stairs.

Goulart stood in the middle of his gigantic reception room, a grim expression on his face.

"Good morning, Mr. Ambassador," he said.

"Good morning, Mr. President."

"It's quite a rain. But it often rains in March."

"In the United States, it's more likely to be April. There's even a song, 'When April showers, they come your way; they bring the flowers that bloom in May.'"

"Tom Jobim wrote a song here in Brazil, Vinicius wrote the lyrics: 'It's the waters of March, ending the summer. . . .'"

Carter knew that both he and the president loved bossa nova. He had, in fact, met Jobim at a party at the presidential palace hosted by Goulart himself. Both Jobim and Elis Regina had been there, Jobim at the piano, Elis singing his songs. Carter had loved it. Those had been different times.

Goulart motioned for Carter to follow him onto the balcony. There was no possibility of hidden microphones outside.

"The news hasn't been good." Goulart said. "It looks like General Cordel may be turning against me, although so far he seems to be opposed to a military coup. He's a good man, and believes in our constitution. He knows I am the democratically elected president of Brazil. But a lot depends on your government. If the United States keeps out of our affairs, I think I can see it through. If not. . . . "

"You know that United States policy is made in Washington on this one, Joao. Not at the embassy."

"Well, what do they want?"

Carter paused. But he really had no choice. "They want you to sever all ties with Luiz Carlos Prestes and the labor movement," he said.

"What else?"

Carter looked down, and noticed that his shoes needed shining. "Basically, they want you to fire your entire cabinet. Your best bet might be to appoint Senator Tancredo Neves your vice president, then leave the country for a while so he can be acting president while things cool down." Neves was the widely respected president of the Chamber of Deputies.

"Anything else?"

Since yesterday Carter had been thinking about whether he should pass Washington's veiled threat on to Goulart. For now, he concluded, it would be better not to.

"Nothing else," he said.

There was a long silence.

"Who *is* making US policy on this?" Goulart asked.

"Well, it isn't just one person. There's a group headed by the secretary of state. It includes the undersecretary of state, the assistant secretary for inter-American affairs, the secretary of defense, the director of the CIA, the national security advisor, and one or two more."

"They must think I'm pretty important," Goulart said.

"You are," Carter said.

"Is your president involved?"

"Very likely."

Goulart turned and looked straight at Carter. There was fire in his eyes and, for the first time, Carter thought, he actually looked presidential.

"Well, you can tell Mr. Johnson," Jango said in English, "from one cowboy president to another, that he can shove his ultimatum up his big fat Texas ass."

"Yes, Mr. President," Carter said.

By the time he arrived back at the embassy, he had drafted his report of the meeting in his head. He wrote it in longhand in his office.

TOP SECRET

Re: Your cable 136/64 yesterday

AMB met today with President Goulart. I conveyed to the president, as gently as possible, our demands regarding severance of his ties with Prestes and the Brazilian labor movement, as well as the dismissal of his cabinet.

He inquired who made policy on this matter for the United States, and asked whether the president was involved. I described the National Security Council and I told him very likely the president was involved. He asked me to forcefully convey to the president that our proposal was not acceptable.

—Carter

Carter walked out of his office and handed the draft to Joannie. Shorter is better, he thought.

"Type that for me, would you," he said to Joannie.

It took her about two minutes. Carter read the draft, then read it again.

"Oh, what the hell," he said to himself. The big boss might even like it. He struck out the last sentence of the draft, and wrote in "He asked me to tell the president, from one cowboy president to another, that he can shove his ultimatum up his big, fat Texas ass."

Carter took the draft back out to Joannie.

"Send this," he said, "before I can change my mind again."

Lyndon Baines Johnson, the thirty-sixth president of the United States of America, still in his pajamas, sat at his breakfast table enjoying his bacon and eggs. In front of him on the table lay the usual pile of cables in during the night from the American embassies all over the world, carefully screened by the State Department and White House staffs, and found to be worthy of his attention. With a sigh, he finished off the last scrap of bacon and turned his attention to the pile.

The first cable, reporting the death in an air crash of the consul general in Libya, he quickly discarded. The second, however, from the American ambassador in Rio de Janeiro, he read with care. Reaching the last sentence, a broad grin crossed his face, then exploded into uproarious laughter.

This guy's got guts, Johnson said to himself. Real guts. We could use a guy like that around here. He sighed. But that's just the kind of guy we *don't* need on the other side.

He clicked the intercom on. "Get me John McCone," he said.

The director of the CIA was on the phone a moment later.

"Good morning, Mr. President, nice weather this morning."

Johnson had no patience for pleasantries. "Have you seen Carter's cable from Rio this morning?"

"Yes sir, I have. Goulart is a rude but courageous man, sir. The cable confirms what our people in the field have already reported. He won't give up easily."

"So?"

"So, I'm afraid he could remain a threat even after the coup. We're pretty sure that with the help you authorized, the Brazilian military will prevail, but they are likely to only banish him from Brazil, not eliminate him. That's not the Brazilian way. They'll probably let him fly to Uruguay, and he and his brother-in-law will go on plotting from there. There's a risk that they could roll back the restoration of democracy that the military will achieve in the coup."

"Who's his brother-in-law?"

"Lionel Brizola, sir, a rabble-rousing Communist governor of Rio Grande do Sul, the Brazilian state closest to Argentina."

"So what do you recommend?"

"I'm afraid it's Plan B," McCone said.

"What does Werner say?"

"He regrets it, sir, but he seems to be in favor of Plan B."

"State?"

"Well, Secretary Rusk has some hesitation, but Mahon thinks we should proceed with Plan B as quickly as possible. Mahon is. . . . "

"I know who he is. He's that little fascist assistant secretary for IAA. He likes killing."

McCone remained silent.

"Carter?"

"He's not cleared for Plan B, sir. I believe he doesn't know. Mr. Mahon believes. . . . "

Johnson looked again at Carter's cable. "I hate agreeing with Mahon," he said, "but this time I think that little prick's got it right. Can we trust your guy in Rio not to fuck it up?"

"He's one of our best," McCone said.

"Okay," the president said, "We go with Plan B. Let Rio station carry it out. Carter doesn't have to know." Too bad, he thought, as he clicked off the phone. From one cowboy president to another. . . . He folded Carter's cable in half and laid it gently in the outbox.

CHAPTER 13

Carter was getting ready to leave the office and drive the yellow beetle to Copacabana when the red light on his intercom lit up.

"I'm sorry to bother you, Mr. Ambassador," Joannie said. "But I have the Soviet embassy on the line. Ambassador Sverdlov wants to meet with you urgently."

"Tell them I've gone home," Carter said.

"I tried that but they say it's extremely urgent and that it has to be today."

Carter sighed. "Oh, all right," he said. "Whose turn is it?" He and Sverdlov each suspected that their offices and their cars were bugged, either by each other's government, or by the Brazilians, or both. So they had agreed that if they had to meet in private, it would be in a taxi, preferably one of the big, old, comfortable ones left over from the '40s or early '50s. They traded off flagging a cab and picking up the other near his embassy.

"Your turn, I think," Joannie said.

He was lucky. He flagged down a dark red 1940 Buick sedan on Rua Mexico. A few minutes later he spotted Sverdlov under an umbrella on a street corner a block from his embassy, looking even sourer than usual. Sverdlov stepped quickly into the cab and sat down next to Carter.

"Leblon," he said to the driver. "Rua Rita Ludolf."

It was about as far from the Soviet embassy as you could get and still be in the South Zone, the wealthy part of Rio where at least some of the streets might be passable in the rain. The Soviets had a safe house on Rita Ludolf.

"Good afternoon, Ivan," Carter said. "If we're going that far, I guess we're in for a long talk. May I know the subject?"

"You know subject," Sverdlov said. "And I want you to know that this time there's not chance in hell you will get away with it."

Carter detected a tremor of rage in the voice of the large Russian diplomat sitting next to him. His beard seemed to be slightly trembling. Carter could guess at the source of the Russian's anger, but decided to play the innocent.

"Get away with what, Mr. Ambassador?" he said.

Sverdlov turned and stared into Carter's eyes. "You know damn well," he said. "It's your flotilla," he said. "Your government is planning to invade Brazil . . . and that we cannot permit."

Carter wasn't surprised that the Russians knew. Of course they would know. Twelve American warships steaming south through international waters off South America would be hard to miss, even if the Russians did not have the world's largest fleet of submarines cruising the oceans and keeping an eye on what was going on. But they did. If Washington hadn't thought of that, Washington was run by fools.

"There's not going to be an invasion, Ivan," he said. "It's just for show, if the government invites us in."

Sverdlov scowled. "Sure," he said, "Jango's going to invite you in. Makes for great show, since he's invited *us* already. Your flotilla is not going to enter Brazilian waters afloat, I can assure you of that. We have submarines, you know, and nuclear warheads."

Carter could feel the back of his neck turn cold. "Ivan," he said softly, "are you threatening to sink warships of the United States Navy?"

"I'm not threatening anything. The threats are being made by your government, not mine. Sending your flotilla is the threat. What could be more threatening than sending twelve warships against a defenseless third world country? It's more than a threat. It is practically an act of war."

He was right, of course, Carter thought. But to sink an American ship would be an act of war against the United States, not Brazil. And this was a threat he had to answer.

"Ivan," he said, "if one of your subs sinks one of our ships, our two countries will be at war—possibly nuclear war."

"Perhaps," Sverdlov said. "But ours is great country. Your president humiliated our president less than two years ago over our legal right to send our missiles to Cuba. Very well, we blinked once. But we will not blink again. We will take whatever measures are required to defend our Brazilian friends against attack. Your warships will enter Brazilian waters at their peril."

Carter looked out the window of the cab at a young Brazilian couple locked in an embrace and a kiss on the street corner in the rain. What he needed was Marina's warm body snuggled next to his own.

"I can't stop them," Carter said. "Your president needs to talk with ours."

Sverdlov snorted. "That's what we tried to do in Cuba. We tried to make a reasonable compromise. You know what happened. The premier will not make the same mistake again."

"I have no authority. . . . "

Sverdlov cut him off. "Well, get authority, Mr. Ambassador, and get it quick."

There was no point in continuing his conversation with Sverdlov. Washington got the United States into this mess, Carter thought. Let them get us back out.

"Driver," Carter said in Portuguese, "you can turn on Rua Paissandu and head back downtown. I'll leave you off at your embassy, Ivan," he said to the Russian glowering next to him. "I hear your message. I am sure you have heard mine. I assure you that Washington will be informed."

It was almost eight o'clock by the time he got back to the embassy.

Joannie had left, apparently thinking he would not return. The office seemed lonely without her. Or maybe it was the thought of what might happen to the world if both countries made good on their threats. Washington must have thought of the risk. Or had it? Or was this just another move in the game of who could push the other further before one of them blew up the world? Was his president trying to show he was just as tough as JFK, or maybe tougher? In any event, Washington clearly didn't want him to know what was going on, much less what he thought should be done. But he would tell them his opinion nevertheless. He was the United States ambassador and that was his job. Carter turned to the typewriter on the table next to his desk.

"Top Secret," he wrote.

To: SecState from AMB

I met this afternoon, at his request, with Soviet Ambassador Ivan Sverdlov. Sverdlov had learned of Operation Brother Sam (I do not know how) and was enraged at what he perceived to be a potential invasion of Brazil by the United States, something he said the Soviet Union could not tolerate. I denied that an invasion was planned, and stated that the flotilla was intended merely as a show of force, if invited in by the Brazilian government. Sverdlov replied this was unlikely since his government had already been invited in. He "assured" me that our ships would not enter Brazilian waters afloat. I inquired directly if he was threatening to sink warships of the US Navy. He denied making a threat, and asserted that it was Operation Brother Sam that was the threat, virtually an act of war. He also pointed out that Soviet submarines were armed with nuclear warheads.

I advised Sverdlov clearly that if one of their subs were to sink one of our ships, it was certain to mean war. Sverdlov replied that while the Soviets had blinked first in the Cuban missile crisis, they would not do so again, and would do whatever was needed to defend Brazil against attack. He seemed to believe that entry by our ships in Brazilian waters would be tantamount to an attack. He suggested that after Cuba, his premier was unwilling to deal with the president, and demanded that I obtain authority to deal with USSR on his behalf.

At this point, the stakes have clearly been raised, and we are talking not only of the political situation of Brazil, but of the potential for serious conflict, perhaps nuclear, with the Soviet Union. I believe that Ambassador Sverdlov was entirely serious, and believes that his country cannot afford to back down again, so soon after the Cuban missile crisis. Although he did not say so, it seems clear he is taking his orders from Moscow.

I believe that Operation Brother Sam is unnecessary and unwise. A coup by the Brazilian military is a virtual certainty, and seems likely to succeed, with or without our military support. Arrival here of an American flotilla, including an aircraft carrier and aircraft, would only be seen here, and throughout the hemisphere, as an interference in Brazil's sovereignty and internal affairs, and might even bring President Goulart and the generals back together in a united front against perceived American imperialism. It could undo all of the goodwill painstakingly created here, and throughout the hemisphere, by President Kennedy and by the Alliance for Progress.

I recommend that the president direct the Brother Sam flotilla to return home, or at least halt its southward progress and remain on hold wherever it may now be located, pending further orders by the president. In any case, its existence must be kept secret, both from President Goulart's government, and from the Brazilian generals. What further communication should be made with the government of the Soviet Union is obviously a question beyond my competence.

Any such communication must be made by Washington, not this
embassy. I have told Ambassador Sverdlov that I had no authority
to represent the United States in this matter and that Washington
would be informed.

Carter read his cable over a few times. There was no doubt it
would leave the Desk furious. Mahon was sure not to like it He was
less sure of the reaction of the secretary of state. But in the end he
walked down to the cable room, woke up the embarrassed cable operator asleep at his desk, and watched him send it off.

Carter walked back to his private elevator and rode it down to
the garage. "Let's go to Posto 6," he said to Joazinho, without thinking.
"And take those flags off the car, please."

His driver looked at him, surprised. "No, I'm not meeting anyone," he said. "I just need a drink. Leave me around the block from the
beach on Nossa Senhora de Copacabana. I'll walk from there."

CHAPTER 14

Guilherme was bringing his caipirinha almost before he sat down. "Haven't seen her," he said, although Carter hadn't asked. "But I'll bet she'll be here soon."

Ten minutes later, she was.

It landed on him the moment he saw her walking up Avenida Atlantica toward him. Last night had been like nothing he ever felt before. She had asked him to make believe he loved her. He didn't have to do that. He *did* love her. Or did he? They had made love in the water and the moonlight, not like the incredible sex of the first lessons she taught him, but something very different. He had come in her with an explosion—he could still feel it now—but gently delicious at the same time.

Marina walked up to his table and grinned. "Hello, Tony," she said. "What are you doing here so late at night?"

"Guess."

"You're looking for me."

"Right."

"And you want to make love again, right now and for free."

"Right again."

"And what makes you think I want to do something like that?"

"I don't know," Carter said. "Maybe because I love you." My God, he thought, I've told a prostitute I love her.

The moonlight sparkled on the water as they walked barefoot down Copacabana Beach, here and there a young couple making love on the sand.

"I used to do that when I was young," Marina said.

"How old were you?"

"Seventeen," Marina said. "But if you'd rather have me be twenty, I'm willing to lie a little."

"Do your customers prefer you to be twenty?"

"Depends on how old they are. Up to forty, they'd rather I was twenty. After that, they seem to like twenty-five better."

"So you tell them what they want to hear."

She nodded.

They walked on down the beach. "Do you do that with me, too?" Carter asked.

"Do what?"

"Lie. Tell me what you think I want to hear."

"Like what?"

"Like that you love me."

"I haven't told you that, Tony."

"I know."

"Oh Tony, don't start. . . . "

He thought he saw tears at the back of her eyes.

"Don't start. I can't stand it, not from you. All those little boys who have asked me: Do I love them? How can I stand to make love for money, how can I call that love, how miserable I must be, how they can rescue me from the street. Are *you* thinking I can't love you, Tony, just because I'm a streetwalker? I don't know whether I can love you. I don't really know what love is. And you don't know whether you love me either, or whether you are just infatuated with the idea, and with me, but scared that you, the ambassador of the United States of America, may be in love with a Brazilian whore." And then the flood-gates opened and she fell into tears on his shoulder.

"Let's go to your apartment," Carter said. "Maybe we'll both learn something."

Marina smiled up at him. "You know," she said, "you really are a sweet man."

CHAPTER 15

Harry Martoni stood at the window of his office on the Praça Maua watching the whores and a few sailors walking through the square. Harry liked watching the square at five a.m. If he stood on his tip-toes, he could see the girls leaving the Hotel Bleqaute across the way, adjusting their blouses and their miniskirts, and a few minutes later, the johns, unkempt, often a bit drunk, and always the worse for wear. Sometimes he could see one of the locals skillfully lifting the wallet from the ass pocket of one of the johns as he walked through the square. He enjoyed that. He liked seeing someone do his work well.

But this morning none of this mattered. He looked down at the cable in his hand, and read it again.

TOP SECRET
3/26/64, Washington FLASH
EYES ONLY for Station Chief Martoni
No distribution

Per your prior recommendation and upon consideration of board of directors, it has been concluded that Red Fox presents clear and present danger to the welfare of Brazil and to ourselves. Accordingly, in connection with the presently anticipated events in Brazil, steps must be taken to assure that Red Fox will not interfere with those events, nor with any similar events that may be required in Brazil in the future.

As this risk must be eliminated, Plan B has been authorized at the highest level USG. You are appointed designated field officer (DFO) for this operation and as such you are authorized to take any action required to achieve the designated objective. Code Green is April 1.

Regards,
McCone

They had finally taken his recommendations, *his* recommendations, which he had sent up repeatedly by cable, and which he thought they had ignored. Instead the National Security Council— the "board of directors"—had considered what he had recommended. His recommendations had been approved at the highest level. "Highest level USG" the cable said. That meant the president! And they had put the whole operation in his hands. He, Harry Martoni, was "authorized to take any action required to achieve the designated objective."

The designated objective was the assassination of Joao Goulart. That was Plan B. There was no other way to make sure there could be no counter-coup that would put him back in the saddle more firmly than ever, like President Janio Quadros thought would happen when he resigned the presidency in 1962. No, there was no doubt: Goulart must not survive the coup. But his personal charm and honesty made it very unlikely that he would be murdered by the Brazilian military. Banished yes, but not executed. That essential task was left for the Agency to carry out, for the good of the United States, Brazil, and the world. And Harry was going to be the one who would do it. That would put him well on his way up, at least to the position of deputy director of the Agency! Or maybe even beyond!

The Code Green date was April 1. He knew that the Agency preferred to carry out this kind of operation a day or two before the coup. That way, Jango would be out of the way and there would be no time for public reaction to crystallize against it before the coup began. So the coup must be scheduled for April 2. He wondered how they knew that, but it didn't really matter. His date with Jango would be April 1, April Fools' Day. That was fine with him. It gave him a few days to prepare.

Goulart was in Rio, at the Laranjeiros Palace. He liked to walk out on his balcony from time to time. That would give Harry an opportunity for a good shot. Or maybe it would be better to take him out in the car, on his way into or out of the palace. Harry would just have to check it all out.

Outside the window the rain seemed to be slowing down a bit. The last stragglers were coming out of the Bleqaute into the early light of the day. Harry's gaze focused on a middle-aged man, his arm around a young, suntanned boy in jeans, perhaps seventeen, as they came out of the hotel and walked across the square. He felt a slight tingle between his legs. He watched them walk across the square and down Rua Sacadura Cabral until they turned into Avenida Rio Branco and disappeared from view.

CHAPTER 16

Carter and Marina made love at her apartment, but it wasn't good. They were in Carter's favorite position, with him on his back and Marina riding on top where he could see her sensuous lips, her gorgeous brown body, and the darker nipples of her breasts, her pubic hair intertwined with his own, she riding him like on a bucking stallion. But tonight it didn't work. For an instant, her pubic hair turned into Sverdlov's beard, then switched back into reality. Then, for a brief moment, his penis, deep inside her, turned into a torpedo speeding toward its target, then became part of him again. In the end, rather than just losing his erection, he pretended an orgasm, and lay back on the pillow panting.

Marina climbed down off him. "Don't ever try to fool me," she said. "I know all about faking. I was a professional, remember?"

"I'm sorry," he said.

"Sure, you're sorry," she said. "Sure you are. It's the damn coup, isn't it? Everyone knows it's coming. But it's *their* coup, not yours. You let it eat you up anyway and take you away from me. You care more about those politicians and generals than you do about me."

"That's not true," he said.

"Maybe it's only a little bit true," Marina said, "but it can't be true at all if you love me."

"I promise I'll never mention the word 'coup' ever again once it happens," Carter said. "I'll be only yours."

"When will that be?"

"I don't know," Carter said. "I wish I did."

Marina was silent for a moment. "Well, suppose you did know?" she asked.

"There's no way I can find out," Carter said. "It's just as you said, it's not my coup."

"Well, I'm going to find out," Marina said. "You're a gringo. It's more my coup than yours. But first, I have to go to the factory and see if it's still there after all the rain. After that I'll find out."

Carter smiled.

"Can you come with me?" Marina asked.

"I'd love to, darling, but I can't. There are some really important cables that will probably be coming in, and I need to be at the embassy to deal with them." Or perhaps a nuclear war, he thought.

"Tomorrow's Saturday," she said.

"I know," he said, although in fact he had forgotten. "But that doesn't matter. I'm the ambassador. There are no days off for the American ambassador when Brazil is about to be in the middle of a military coup."

He knew he'd made a mistake the moment he mentioned the word "coup." She glared at him. "You've never been to my little factory. Not once. You are just 'too busy' with the generals. All right, have a good time. I'm going to the factory. You can do whatever you like." She left in the morning without kissing him goodbye.

Carter got dressed in the living room and went downstairs to find the VW. He couldn't remember where he had parked the night before until it occurred to him that he had left it at the embassy. For the first time ever, he had gone to the Bar Atlantico in the Cadillac. Joazinho had driven it back to the embassy. So he'd have to take a taxi to the embassy. He looked out the door up and down the street. There were no taxis in sight. The rain was still falling and the brown river was still running down the middle of Siqueira Campos. In fact, there were no cars at all, other than an old Plymouth sedan parked a ways up the street. "Damn," Carter said under his breath. He walked back upstairs and called the motor pool on Marina's phone.

Somehow, Joaozinho arrived in the Cadillac in less than half an hour. Carter walked quickly out from under the concrete canopy of the building, skipped over a large puddle, and climbed into the back seat. He did not notice that the front window on the driver's side of the Plymouth had been rolled down and a long lens was pointed in his direction.

It was after eleven o'clock when Carter arrived at the embassy. He greeted the marine guard in his slightly ridiculous white dress uniform, and took his private elevator to the seventh floor.

The Desk had been bugging his admin section about the February personnel ratings. Carter was supposed to review and approve them, and the section chief was begging him to do it before the Desk drove him crazy. The personnel ratings could determine a foreign service officer's entire future, Carter knew. He spent the next two hours reviewing them.

Then there was that idiot John O'Toole from Westinghouse do Brasil who had demanded an appointment yesterday. O'Toole's only claim to fame was his friendship with Senator Thomas Scheisser of Ohio, for whom O'Toole had raised some $3 million in the last election. Scheisser was chairman of the Senate Foreign Relations Committee. "Better play it safe," Carter said to himself. He dictated an apologetic letter to O'Toole into his dictation machine and put the tape on Joannie's desk.

There was, of course, all kinds of other trash: at least six invitations to appear in panel discussions in both Sao Paulo and Rio, mostly on such inane subjects as "The Role of Democracy in Brazil and the Modern World," "Race Relations—Brazil and the US

Compared," and the like. There were requests for interviews from the *Jornal do Brasil* (accept) and from *Ultima Hora* (reject); an invitation to Mrs. Carter to judge a competition of floral arrangements at the Sao Paulo Garden Club. He threw them all in the out box for Joannie to take care of.

Carter was still at his desk when Washington's response to his cable arrived. Carter hadn't expected a reply quite so soon, but he wasn't really surprised. They had made up their minds long ago. They didn't want to hear now that they might be wrong.

TOP SECRET

SECSTATE 327/64
Ref your Amb 57/64
For Ambassador
No distribution

We have received and carefully considered your arguments contained REFTEL. Embassy may not fully appreciate the importance of a victory by Brazilian democratic military forces against radical Communist government for the preservation of democracy in both Brazil and the hemisphere. Operation Brother Sam, which has been authorized at the highest level USG, will provide essential support to the Brazilian military if we decide such support is needed. The Operation is essential to assure the furtherance of our interests and to preservation of democracy in the hemisphere. It cannot be cancelled or delayed.

You are correct that any contacts with the Soviets regarding Brother Sam are beyond competence of your embassy. Embassy shall refrain from speaking further to the Soviets regarding Brother Sam, and shall have no further involvement, direct or indirect, with that Operation. All aspects of the Operation are being decided in

*Washington. Brother Sam is classified top secret, and shall not
be revealed beyond those in Washington who are directly involved.
We are, in fact, somewhat concerned that existence of Operation
Brother Sam has even become known to embassy. Please report
immediately the source of your information.*

Regards,
Rusk

Carter could tell right away that the Desk had written it. He
turned and looked up at the benignly smiling official photograph
of LBJ on the wall behind his desk. "They're scared pissless, Mr.
President," he said. "And so am I. They only care about protecting
their own asses. There's a lot more at stake here than that: Brother
Sam has to be stopped, Mr. President. Damned if I know how, but it's
got to be stopped . . . before it blows up the world."

The night watchman stood in Joannie's office, at the edge of the
glass door which separated the ambassador's office from hers, and
watched Carter speaking to the picture on the wall. He's snapped, he
thought, he's gone completely around the bend. As we Brazilians say,
he has gone permanently crazy.

It was after one o'clock in the morning by the time he got back to
the residence. There was a message on his bed. "Tony," it read, "I am
going home. This place is not for me. And you are not for me any more.
I'm sorry. Priscilla."

So am I, he thought. Or was that too a lie?

CHAPTER 17

It had taken Marina four buses and a little over three hours to make it from Copacabana to Bangu. The first took her from Siqueira Campos to the Rodoviaria, Rio's central bus station. The second went from the Rodoviaria to Freguesia in Jacarepagua, where she changed to the bus for Bangu. From the center of Bangu, she took the local bus to the Women's Penitentiary. She had managed to buy a small piece of land, 150 square meters, just outside the prison walls, and install her factory there. People were afraid of possible prison breaks, so the land was cheap. Her brother arranged for a few of his fellow construction workers to put up a simple one-story building out of cinder block. He also knew how to tap into the overhead power line, so she had electricity for free. All that was missing were the sewing machines and those, as she had told Carter long ago, she had earned on her back.

Marina was, in fact, one of the leading entrepreneurs of Bangu. Unlike the large businesses along the main road out of Rio, many owned by gringos from the U.S. or Europe, she paid her workers the legally required minimum wage and signed the labor cards that entitled them to social security and public health. She didn't want her employees having to work on their backs, or for their kids to work as runners for the drug trade that was just getting started in the favelas. Of course, neither she nor anyone else in the favelas paid any taxes.

Why should they? The government did nothing for them. Besides, they couldn't afford it. Marina had, however, been one of the first contributors to the Bangu Protective Association, an informal association of businesses and homeowners that protected the favela by the simple expedient of executing any killer, thief, or drug dealer who lived there, or tried to. The association knew who they were. There was no need for a trial.

Eleninha, Marina's sister and the factory manager, hurried over to greet her. There was a new order for infant pajamas from Mesbla, the largest department store in Rio, but they had to be delivered by Thursday and only three of the machines were working. The girls were working around the clock, Eleninha said, but there was no way to complete the order by Thursday without all four machines working.

"What's wrong with the fourth?" Marina asked.

"I don't know," Eleninha said. "I think it's the rain. Some water must have gotten into the motor."

"Never mind," Marina said. "I suppose I could go back to Jorge Bastos's store in Freguesia. Maybe he'll give us credit for a new machine."

Jose Henrique had the only appliance store in all of Jacarepagua. He sold Singer machines, and she knew he would give her credit. But the price was too high: Jose Henrique was fat, never washed, and smelled of sweat, glands, garlic, and the cheap cigars he smoked. The interest rate for credit from Jose Henrique was a minimum of two tricks a week, plus a blow job on Sunday. She couldn't bring herself to do it even before she became Carter's lover. Certainly she couldn't do it now.

"What would be the cheapest machine we could get for cash?" she asked Eleninha.

"I checked," said Eleninha. "You can buy a Sears for $110." She couldn't make that in a week, Marina thought. Maybe Anthony would lend it to her. Or even give it to her. But the anger started up all over again, in her throat and in the depth of her stomach. He could be here, helping her with the accounts, solving her problems, helping her business survive; instead he was too busy playing "coup" with the generals and the politicians.

"Fuck you, Anthony," she said out loud.

The afternoon sun was starting to go down when she first felt Jean Pierre's eyes focused on her ass. It wasn't unusual. Like the rest of her, her ass was near perfect. Brazilians were partial to *bundas*, as bottoms were called. It was not unusual for her to feel their eyes, or even their hands, lightly stroking her ass as she walked down the street.

But it *was* unusual to have a pair of arms embrace her from behind, to feel a male body pressed up against her, and a French voice whisper in her ear "*Aló* Marina."

She had not seen Jean Pierre in over a year. She remembered him as tall and slim, young and handsome (as the Tom Jobim song almost went) with a shock of sandy-colored hair that fell forward over his sunburned face. He wasn't bad in bed and she might even have liked him if he hadn't drunk so much, and then turned maudlin and felt desperately sorry for himself. His best points were that he always paid her $50 in US dollars in advance without her even asking, and he always fell asleep right after sex, which allowed her to duck out of the motel without a lot of boring conversation.

She turned to face him.

"Well, sweetheart, where have you been?" He looked older and tired. His complexion had turned just a little pasty, his breath smelled of *cachaça*, garlic, and cheese.

"Oh, away," he said. "I've been sick."

"VD?"

"Oh no, nothing like that. . . . I need you. That's why I tracked you out here. I need you," he said again. He leaned his head forward and whispered into her ear, "$100."

The sewing machine cost $110. Tony was off playing ambassador somewhere, worrying about the damn "coup" instead of her. But. . . .

"No," she said.

"Why not?" Jean Pierre's voice was pleading. "$100," he said again. "That's double our old arrangement."

"Because I have given up that sort of business. My body's not for rent any more."

The Frenchman looked at her. There was a long pause. "$200," he said.

$200! That was almost two sewing machines, a fifty percent increase in capacity. It would solve the Mesbla problem and then some. She was Tony's woman. She loved him. But. . . .

"Hell," she said inside. "Love is love, and business is business." She started walking briskly toward the office door at the back of the factory.

"Come on," she said to the Frenchman. "But it's only one trick. And no blow job."

CHAPTER 18

The photos arrived at Carter's office mid-afternoon in a brown paper envelope marked "Ambassador Carter—Personal." The marine guard reported that it had been handed to him by a swarthy bald Brazilian who appeared to be a taxi driver. He had taken it upstairs and put it on the ambassador's desk.

Carter opened it when he returned from lunch. The first one was a picture of Carter carrying his attaché case, coming out of a nondescript gray building and stepping over a large puddle in the rain. He recognized it as Marina's building. Next to the doorway was a small plaque bearing the number 153. In the next building down the street was a juice bar, closed, with a sign above the front window that read *"Sucos Siqueira Campos."*

The second photo was taken at the same place, but instead of Carter, there was a tall, stunning mulatta stepping over the same puddle in front of the same building in the rain. She wore a pair of tight black jeans, black high-heeled sandals and a light-colored cardigan sweater which seemed just large enough to tightly cover her breasts and her nipples. No brassiere. She was carrying a white umbrella and a stylish white leather purse on a strap over her shoulder.

"Oh, my God!" he said. "They've got Marina." A stab of panic began to roil his stomach. He closed his eyes and her beautiful brown body came up, and her sparkling eyes, and her lips. "Oh, my God!" he said again.

It took ten minutes before his mind started working rationally again and questions began forming in his mind. If they had her, what did they want? There was no ransom note, no demand he pay anything or take any action, or do anything at all, or not do something. And who were "they"? There was no signature, no indication of who had sent the envelope: the Communists? Someone in the government? The military? Whoever sent it had taken some care to make sure he wouldn't know who had sent it. And why the photo of him if the hostage was Marina?

He needed an independent pair of eyes, a second mind, to look with him at the photos and figure out what they meant. But there was no one whom he could safely tell about Marina, at least no one in the American community. He picked up the phone and dialed the Canadian embassy.

"May I speak to Dr. Sprague, please. This is Ambassador Carter."

A moment later his friend was on the line. "Well, Tony," he boomed. "Long time no hear. What's the matter, you come down with the clap?"

"No," said Carter. "It's worse than that."

"Syphilis?"

"Cut that out, Jack. I've got a real problem. Could you drop over here as soon as you can?"

Dr. Sprague was in his office ten minutes later. Carter waved him into a chair.

"Look at these," he said.

Jack picked up the two photos and studied them closely.

"Well," Carter said, "what do you think?"

"May I ask you a few questions first?" Jack asked.

"Go ahead," Carter said. "I want to know what you think. That's why I called you."

"She's the girl who we saw at the Romanian embassy, right?

"Right," Carter said.

"And now she's your girlfriend?"

"Yes," Carter said. "Well, sort of."

"How long?"

"About two weeks," he said, although it seemed a lot longer.

Sprague nodded. "Mrs. Carter doesn't know?"

"She knows. She's gone back home. To Ohio."

"Does your State Department know?"

"I don't think so."

"Or anyone else in Washington?"

"Not that I know of."

"The Russkis?"

"I don't think so, but you never know."

"How about the spooks?"

Carter shrugged.

"You're sleeping together in Copacabana?"

Carter was taken aback. "How do you know about that?" he asked.

"Because you are both coming out of the same building on Siqueira Campos at almost the same time—look at the puddle. . . . It's unchanged in the two pictures. You each look like you're coming out of the same building, both of you with briefcases. And I'll bet 153 Siqueira Campos is an apartment building, not a cheap hotel."

Sprague looked up from the photos. "Somebody has been laying for you, Tony," he said. "Somebody who wants something from you. That's the reason for pictures of each of you in the same place and almost the same time. Anyone who saw them would conclude the two of you spent the night together. That's why they sent you both pictures, not just hers, just so you would know they know. And if you don't play ball, they'll send them somewhere else as well, like to Priscilla, or to Washington." Sprague paused. "It's a perfect little setup for blackmailing the ambassador of the United States of America," he said. "Couldn't do it better myself."

"But who is it? What do they want?" Carter said. "No one has asked me to do anything."

"I don't know," the doctor said. "Maybe they want you to do nothing. I expect you'll find out pretty soon. They'll let you know."

"They? Who's 'they'? I have no idea whether it's the Communists or Jango's people, or the Russians, or God knows who."

"Neither do I. Maybe it's your own spooks."

Carter stared at him. "That can't be," he said. "We may not get along that well, but we're all part of the United States government, the same team. The CIA wouldn't try to blackmail the United States ambassador, the head of the country team. . . . "

"I expect they've done worse than that," Sprague said.

What did that mean? Carter wondered. Suddenly the panic rose up in his stomach again.

"You don't think anyone's kidnapped Marina, do you, Jack?"

"No," Sprague said. "That would be too messy. And why try to spirit her away if knowing she exists and that she's your girlfriend can be just as valuable or more so, if they can prove it." He picked up the photographs. "And these prove it."

"So, what would you do next?"

"I don't know," Sprague said. "I guess I'd just wait and see what *they* do next."

Sprague was almost out the door when Carter stopped him. "Jack, you're not a spook yourself, are you?"

The doctor grinned. "Mr. Ambassador," he said with a fairly good imitation of a Russian accent, "One never knows, do one?" He winked and was gone.

CHAPTER 19

Harry stood in his window looking down on the square. Although it was four in the morning, the sky was already turning from black to gray. A few streaks of pink spread above the office buildings in Niteroi across the bay. It's going to be a hot day, Harry thought. Hell, it always was.

Harry let his eyes wander over the square. A sailor was necking with a whore outside the Pussycat Lounge. An older gringo and a teenage girl were emerging from the Bleqaute across the way. An orange-clad street sweeper was sweeping up the detritus of the night.

And then he saw her. Marina was standing under one of the two unbroken streetlights in the square, smoking a cigarette. Harry gasped. He grabbed his binoculars and looked closer. Yes, it *was* her. She was wearing a very short pair of hot pants over her black panty-hose. On top she had on a tight black see-through blouse. He couldn't be sure if she was wearing a brassiere. In any case, he could make out the shape of her nipples pressing against her blouse. She had fucked him once—years ago when she was sixteen and only charged 100 cruzeiros. She had changed. No longer the gorgeous little sex kitten she was back then. But he was sure she was the same person with whom he had spent an unbelievable night, the best of his life, some years ago, and who had then disappeared into the night trade in Copacabana. Only she was even more beautiful now. He snapped off the light and raced for the elevator. The goddamn thing seemed to take an hour to get him down to the street. He needn't have worried. She was still there.

Harry hurried across the square. "Hi, honey," he said. "Remember me? From years ago, out here in the square? How about a drink?"

Marina smiled. "Sure I do," she said. "Why not?"

The Pussycat Lounge was still open (it closed only from nine to ten a.m. for cleaning). They were the only customers.

"Scotch, please, Felipe," Marina called to the bartender. "Red Label."

Harry knew the drill. Of course it was tea, but he didn't care. He could feel himself already getting hard under the table.

"I haven't seen you around the square," he said.

"I haven't been here. I've been busy."

"With anyone in particular?"

"Sure," Marina said. "Is there anyone who's in general? Actually, it's the other way around. It's the generals who would like to be in me, only I won't let them."

Harry laughed. "You know what I mean," he said.

Marina blushed. She had learned how to blush at will from the madam of the Pink House.

"You are Ambassador Carter's friend now, aren't you?"

"How do you know?"

"I work in the embassy," Harry said. "I know."

"I'm not his girlfriend any more. He doesn't love me, he can go to hell!"

Harry gazed at the gorgeous mulatta sitting in front of him. It didn't sound quite right, but who cared? He was going to screw the ambassador's girlfriend! Besides, his balls were beginning to hurt.

"Let's go fuck," he said to Marina.

"Sure," she said. "Let's go."

The rooms at the Bleqaute were small with two tiny night tables, a simple black wrought iron double bed and a mirror. The sheets were dingy but clean. Marina knew the rooms well; she had been in the Bleqaute before.

"Wait here," she said to Harry.

He stood and watched her duck into the bathroom and shut the door. It seemed an eternity until the door opened again and Marina came out, stark naked.

Harry gasped. She was, without any doubt, the most beautiful woman he had ever seen. Her skin was burnished copper. Her perfect, long legs met in a luscious clump of black pubic hair, which matched the tufts of black hair under her arms. Her breasts were firm and large, with broad, dark brown nipples that seemed ready to burst. The red of her lips perfectly set off the sparkling white of her teeth. And those incredible large, gray-green eyes, perfectly highlighted by mascara, latched onto him and would not let him go. Her gleaming black hair fell down her back almost to her waist. He ached to have her, and moved to take her in his arms.

She began to unbutton his shirt. When it was open, she ran her tongue expertly around his chest, first one nipple and then the other.

"Do you like that?" she asked.

Harry nodded yes, and reached for Marina's breasts.

"Stop that," she said. "I tell you when you can. Now stand over here."

Harry moved over and stood next to the bed. The pants came off next, slipping down his legs to his ankles. She reached her fingers under his briefs and held onto him.

"You forgot my shoes," Harry said.

"No, I didn't. Sit down on the bed," she ordered. "Now spread your legs."

She knelt down with her head between Harry's knees and began to untie his shoes while she moved her lips over his briefs. Harry groaned.

"Can't you take it?" Marina asked mischievously. "Now your underpants. Stand up."

Harry did as he was told. Marina moved in front of him and ever so slowly began pulling down his briefs with her teeth. Harry moved to help her.

"Stop that," Marina said. "Let me do it or I'll go home."

It seemed an age to Harry until the briefs came down to his testicles and his penis popped out. Marina looked at it appreciatively.

"Hmmmmm," she said. "It's big."

With one hand she slid his briefs down to the floor. With the other, she held loosely onto his testicles, while she slipped her lips around his penis.

"Don't move," Marina said. "Don't move at all, or I'll stop."

Harry didn't move.

"Lie down on the bed," Marina ordered. "On your back."

Harry did as he was told, his erection throbbing. Marina opened her purse and took out four silk ties. Anthony's best neckties. But it would be worth it.

"Stretch out your legs," she said to Harry, "and spread them apart."

She took a blue paisley and tied Harry's right ankle to the bottom right bedpost. Next she took an orange-and-black military stripe and tied his left ankle to the bed.

"Okay, arms up," she said.

She used Tony's diplomatic deep red cocktail party tie to bind Harry's right wrist to the top right bedpost. For his left wrist, she chose Tony's green tie with the butterflies. Harry looked a little ridiculous, spread to the four winds, and held there by four gaily colored sails, with a thick mast in the middle.

"How do you feel?" she asked Harry.

"Fine."

"Well, let's make *me* feel fine, too," she said.

She climbed onto the bed and knelt down with her knees on either side of him.

"Now, make me feel good," she said to him. "With your mustache. You know how."

He did know how. In five minutes Marina was feeling as hot as he. This was beginning to be fun, she thought. Remember, Tony, this is all for you. In five minutes more, she came.

When the shaking stopped, she moved her body down Harry's body, and ran her tongue expertly around the inside of his ear.

"Are you ready, Harry?" she asked.

His breath was coming so fast he could not answer.

"No?" she said.

"God, yes!" Harry gasped.

She dropped down just far enough for him to slide an inch inside her, and began to slowly slide her hips up and down. Harry lurched to grab her hips, but the neckties held.

"Be patient, darling," she said, "we'll be there soon."

Harry thrust his hips up and managed to get two inches inside of her.

She dropped her hips just enough to give him three inches inside her. Harry was dripping sweat now and breathing very heavily. His arms and legs pulled against the ties.

"Please, Marina," he begged. "Please."

She looked down at him. Harry was very flushed and breathing hard. A client of hers had once suffered a stroke when she tortured him too long. Better safe than sorry, she thought. She slid all the way onto him and with one hand flicked the neckties off his wrists. Then she began to move, plunging up and down with him deep inside her.

"Now you can move," she said. Her long black hair flew wildly over her back. "Buck me off if you can, Harry! I want to ride!"

Harry came thirty seconds later. Marina faked an orgasm and collapsed on the bed next to him.

"That was fabulous," Harry said. "Fabulous!" He lay quiet for a moment. "When can we do it again?"

"When would you like to?"

"Tomorrow."

"Oh," she said sadly. "I can't tomorrow. I'm having dinner with my mom. How about April 1? April Fools' Day? That would be fun."

Harry looked distraught. "I can't do April 1," he said.

Marina curled her gorgeous lips into a pout. "Why not?" she asked.

"I can't tell you why not," Harry said. "It's work. I just can't."

"April 2, then?" Marina asked.

" No," Harry said. How about April 3 or 4?"

A big smile spread across Marina's face. She had found out what Tony wanted to know. The coup was set for April 2 or maybe the first. That was why Harry was busy until the third, why he couldn't fuck her again until then. "Sure," she said. "The third is great." But in fact she knew he would never fuck her again. From April 3 on, she belonged to Anthony.

"What do I owe you for tonight?" Harry asked.

She stood up and looked down at Harry, sprawled, exhausted and still sweating, across the bed. She thought of the champagne she was going to drink with Tony on April 3. Real French champagne. It was expensive. She didn't know how much, but $200 sounded good.

"$200, US" she said to Harry. "I hope it was worth it."

Harry could barely nod his head yes. He reached over to his pants and took out two hundred dollar bills and slid them over to her. "Yes," he said. "Yes, it was. It was great!"

CHAPTER 20

The Palacio das Laranjeiras, the once-official residence of the president of Brazil, towers above Parque Guinle, a small European-style park reachable through a maze of tiny streets off the Rua das Laranjeiras. The palace itself, a smaller version of the Palace of Versailles, was constructed by the Guinle family in 1913, and served as the family residence and the center of aristocratic life in Brazil until 1940, when the aristocracy fell on hard times and the property was sold to the federal government. In 1954, President Juscelino Kubitchek took it over as his residence. It was still the official residence of the president of the republic when Jango Goulart assumed the presidency in 1962 and promptly moved in.

By that time, a series of three- and four-story apartment buildings had been built along the road across from the palace fronting on the park. The apartments were immensely popular, especially with foreigners living in Rio. Access to the buildings was through an ancient gate at the bottom of the road that was occasionally manned by an unarmed policeman.

Traffic through the park consisted mostly of the president, his staff, visitors to the palace, and the inhabitants of the apartment buildings and their guests. The view from the front of the apartments looked out over the park to the towers of the palace beyond, and reminded the lucky residents of Paris, not Brazil. The gringos loved them: The demand and the rents were both extremely high.

Harry lay on his stomach on the roof of Building C, studying the palace across the park. Next to him lay his Uzi rifle in its soft flannel bag, its parts still separated. He had won the gun in the state marksmanship competition in Virginia ten years ago. It was his most treasured possession.

Harry opened the bag, removed the parts of the gun, and carefully fitted them together. Then he raised the scope to his eye and looked through the crosshairs across the park to the palace. His view above the trees onto the terrace off the presidential suite was perfect; it would be almost too easy. There was a problem, though. In the brightness of the day, he could not see through the windows into the darkness inside. Harry was an excellent marksman, but he could not shoot what he couldn't see.

A delivery truck from the wholesale food market on the Rua das Laranjeiras emerged from behind the palace and started down the road toward him. Near the top of the hill, the road turned to the right and Harry could see the driver perfectly, outlined against the tropical blue sky. Perfect, he said to himself. Inside or outside, it was duck soup. He would get Jango in his car. It would be sure to get him a promotion at the Agency, maybe even to chief of the Latin American division. That would put him above that son of a bitch he worked for now. . . . He couldn't wait for April 1.

His thoughts were interrupted by the unwelcome sound of a helicopter above the other buildings farther up the hill. Quickly, he picked up the gun and its bag and hurried over to the door that took him off the roof, and down the stairs to his car.

It took him less than half an hour to drive back to the Praça Maua. How could he have been so stupid? Yes, it was a perfect shot. But of course the palace would be guarded by helicopters, and there was no way of knowing whether the crew of the chopper was for Jango or against him. In any case, it was important that they not be able to tell where the fatal shot came from. They hadn't been able to pinpoint the source of the shot that killed Kennedy. If the FBI couldn't figure that out, for sure the Brazilians wouldn't be able to tell who shot Jango. . . . Unless, of course, they saw him. The solution was obvious: He would have to shoot from inside one of the apartments, not from the roof.

As soon as he arrived at his office, Harry ordered his secretary to get his mole in the admin section of the embassy to make a list of all the embassy and embassy-related personnel who had apartments in Parque Guinle, and on what floors. She should find out the size of the families as well, and whether there were any kids. It shouldn't be difficult.

In fact, it was not difficult at all. By the time Harry came back from lunch, she had the answers. There were eighteen embassy families with apartments at Parque Guinle. Of these, eleven had apartments on the first or second floors. There were seven with apartments on the third or fourth floors. Six of these were occupied by families with two or three kids. Someone would always be there. The seventh, apartment 401 in Bloco B, was occupied by a bachelor, Peter J. Thornton, the USAID legal advisor.

Harry's heart pounded. He was truly on a roll. Not only would he himself be carrying out Plan B, he would be using that little prick lawyer's apartment to do it. If they trace the bullet, that's where they would trace it to. He'd need just a little bit of help. Harry picked up his phone and dialed Oscar Cavalcanti. The general answered the phone himself.

"Oscar," Harry said in Portuguese. "It's Harry."

"I know who it is," Cavalcanti said. "I could tell that gringo accent anywhere. And you always call at lunchtime."

Harry was sure he had no accent in Portuguese at all, but he decided to let that pass. And Oscar was obviously back from lunch.

"You remember that business about the prods?"

"Sure I do."

"Well, I need a little help. Could you drop by sometime today? I have some sweets, some *papos de anjo*. I can't eat them all."

"I'll try to come by," said Cavalcanti. He loved *papos de anjo*. He was in Harry's office ten minutes later.

"Sit down, Oscar," Harry said, passing him the pastries. "You remember that little prick legal advisor at the embassy who blew the whistle on the cattle prods?"

The general looked puzzled. "What whistle?" he said.

"Oh, never mind," Harry said. "He screwed up the delivery with his memo."

Cavalcanti nodded.

"Well, I need to make sure he's tied up somewhere on Monday, then maybe a couple of days later again. Can you handle that?"

"Tied up?"

"Busy."

"Oh," Cavalcanti said. "You mean permanently?"

"No, no, just for the day. And no rough stuff."

The general swatted a fly away from his ear. "That shouldn't be difficult," he said, with evident regret.

An envelope addressed to "Peter J. Thornton, Department Juridical" was delivered to the embassy marine guard by messenger at 3:23 that afternoon. The guard delivered it himself to the legal office on the fourth floor. The paper inside the envelope was clearly an official document of the government of Brazil.

> *Government of the Federative Republic of Brazil*
> *Ministry of Finance*
> *Customs Division*

> **SUMMONS**
> *To Mr. Peter J. Thornton*
> *Legal Advisor*
> *Embassy of the United States of America*

Avenida Presidente Wilson 63
Nesta

Dear Sir:

You are summoned to appear at the offices of the Customs Division,
Ministry of Justice of the Federative Republic of Brazil at Avenida
Rodrigues Alves 1269, Room 242 on Wednesday April 1, 1964,
beginning at 9:30 a.m. to testify at a hearing conducted by this
Division in the matter of Federative Republic of Brasil v. 180
cattle prods. You are requested to bring with you copies of all cor-
respondence and other official documents in your possession relating
to this matter. Additional sessions of the hearing may be required.

The document was signed with an illegible signature over the
title "Director of Customs."

What the hell is this all about? Thornton said to himself. He
knew about the cattle prods, of course. He had written a memo to the
ambassador about them some time ago. But why was the Brazilian
government summoning him to appear at a hearing about the prods?
Anyway, they couldn't summon a member of the embassy staff who
held a diplomatic passport. Under international law, if they didn't like
what he was up to, the only remedy was to declare him persona non
grata. And that, they seemed unlikely to do. He simply would not show
up for the hearing, he thought, but it would be wise to check with the
ambassador. He ran off a copy of the summons and messengered it to
the ambassador's office.

Joannie called him an hour later. "The boss wants to talk with
you. Let me put him on."

Carter's voice came booming over the line a moment later. "What
the hell is this all about, Peter?"

"I don't have any idea, sir," Thornton said. "Of course you know
about the prods."

Carter snorted.

"They're still in customs," Thornton continued, "but I haven't a clue what the hearing's all about. In any case, under international law there is no way they can summon me. I have diplomatic status."

Carter was silent for a moment. "Ignore it," he said. "Better yet, send them a polite note telling them that pursuant to applicable international law, we respectfully decline their invitation." Carter paused again. "And tell them to please go fuck themselves in Mesbla's window, unless you think that might reflect adversely on bilateral relations. Oh hell! Handle it any way you want."

"Yes sir," Thornton said. "Do you think—" but the ambassador had already rung off.

An incoming cable waited in a red envelope on Carter's desk when he returned from lunch.

SECRET
No. 273/64

For Ambassador Carter
From SecState
Re Consultations

In light of rapidly evolving factual scenario please proceed to Washington ASAP for consultations and briefing of president and members of NSC on current developments, and for discussions of next steps to be taken by USG. We will expect you here no later than morning April 1, although your earlier arrival will be appreciated.

Regards,
Rusk

"Shit," Carter thought. Why can't they write English? Like "as soon as possible" instead of ASAP or "National Security Council" instead of NSC or "US government" instead of "USG." Oh, well, that wasn't the worst of it.

The photos had made it pretty obvious that someone was trying to blackmail him, and now his own government was removing him from the scene in Brazil. Of course, the call for "consultations" could be genuine. But Washington hadn't been paying his opinions much attention recently. They had even ordered him to keep his nose out of Brother Sam altogether. Why the sudden interest in his views now?

No, more likely either State or the CIA or both wanted him out of the way so that they could work freely with the Brazilian military in carrying out the coup, and possibly assassinating Jango, without Carter's interference. But who were they planning to put in charge of the embassy while he was away? Theoretically, the DCM would take over, but there was no way they would allow Villepringle to assume command at this critical time. Even the Desk wasn't that stupid. Who would they put in his place? Who asked that the cable be sent?

Carter flicked on his intercom. "Please come in here a moment," he said. Joannie was in his office ten seconds later.

"Joannie, would you please get me a ticket on the Pan Am flight to Washington on April 3. First class."

Joannie looked perplexed. "I peeked at the cable, boss. It says 'ASAP.' I'm sure I can get you a ticket for earlier than April 3."

"Insubordination!" Carter bellowed. "When I say April 3, I mean April 3." He grinned. "The flights tonight, tomorrow, until the third, are all full," he said. "Aren't they?"

"Yes, boss," Joannie said. She started out of his office. "I'll see to it."

Carter stopped her. "I want to dictate a cable to Washington," he said.

"Yes sir."

"Usual classification. For SecState, Eyes only.

1. This acknowledges your cable 273/64. I will book flight to D.C. as soon as possible. I will further inform you when my travel plans are firm.

2. We have completed our investigation regarding source of leak of information regarding Operation Brother Sam, as requested SECSTATE 327/64. I apologize delay due to press of other matters here. There is little question that the source of this information was my military attaché, General Otto Werner. We are unable to inform you with certainty precisely how many additional persons were informed of the operation. I personally doubt that it was more than two or three within the embassy, but that is only surmise on my part. I have also been unable to determine how many, if any, of the Brazilian officer corps sympathetic to our side have been informed.

In any case, I am certain that General Werner was attempting to be helpful. I have no doubt whatsoever of his loyalty to the United States.

I look forward to seeing you soon."

"That's it," Carter said. "Let me see it before it goes out."

"Yes, sir," Joannie said.

Carter sat at his desk, thinking. Actually, Otto may have saved the world by allowing his knowledge of Brother Sam to slip out. But for that, Carter would be completely ignorant of the plan, and the United States and the Soviet Union might not be talking at all. So far, his conversations with Ambassador Sverdlov didn't seem to have made much difference, but at least there was now a channel of communication between their two countries, whether they wanted to listen to each other or not. At this point, though, he didn't even know where the Brother Sam task force was. If he didn't know at least that much, there was little chance the Russians would give his views any attention at all.

His only source of information had been Otto. Very likely he was the one who was trying to get him out of the country so that he could take charge. Obviously, he couldn't rely on any information Otto might give him now. But there might be a way, Carter thought, to get Otto to play it straight with him . . . or at least straighter.

"Joannie, would you bring that draft cable in to me, please? It's not going out just yet. And could you please get me a cup of coffee?"

"Sure, boss," she said.

CHAPTER 21

Marina and Lucia sat on the deck at Castelinho overlooking the ocean in the gathering dusk. Marina loved Castelinho. Unlike the bars she knew in Copacabana, this one, at the beginning of Ipanema, was at the edge of the ocean itself. At high tide it sometimes seemed as if the sea would tear the deck away. But it didn't. The deck, she thought, was itself a marina, like she. And both of them were there to stay. But sometimes she wasn't sure. Like now.

The ocean waves crashed white on the beach and rolled up to the piers which held the deck firm, some ten feet above the sand. The waiter came bearing two caipirinhas. Marina raised the green, frosty glass to her friend.

"Chin, chin," Lucia said quietly, and took a long, cool sip. Lucia had been her best friend for some ten years. They had worked the streets together in Copacabana since they were both sixteen years old. From time to time, they would pick up a couple of guys traveling together and take them both back to Lucia's apartment on Figueredo Magalhaes. The boys would get two for the price of one: After the first screw, the girls would switch and the boys could go at it again. Sometimes, when business was bad, just the two of them would go back to Lucia's apartment together. The sex was good because they were good friends and it was genuine, and it was a lot better than going home alone.

"What's the matter?" Lucia said.

"Nothing."

"Oh, come on, you don't cry over nothing."

"I'm not crying."

"Sure," Lucia said, looking at Marina's eyes. "And the ocean isn't wet, either."

"I can't cry," Marina said. "You can't cry in our business."

"You're not in our business anymore."

A particularly large wave crashed at the surf line just as Marina collapsed into tears.

"Good," said Lucia, "that's good." She moved around the table and put her arm around her. "You're shaking," she said. "Hold onto me."

She stroked Marina's long black hair. "Hold onto me," she said again, "and tell me what's the matter."

Marina looked down the long white beach to where the green ocean crashed ashore at the two huge red rocks of Dois Irmaos—Two Brothers—which closed off the beach at Vidigal. Not two brothers, two sisters, she thought. Like Lucia and me. She stiffened her back. "I'm okay," she said.

Lucia got up and moved back to her side of their little wooden table.

"So?" she said.

"It's Tony," Marina said. "It's been weeks now and all he cares about is the coup. He promised to take me to Buzios. He knows someone with a house there, we could go for the weekend. But then he gets some cable or something, and we can't go." She could feel the tears coming up into her eyes again. "He acts like it's *his* coup, not the generals'." She was crying again.

Lucia reached across the table and squeezed her hand. "It's okay. It's good to cry."

"Then he promised we'd go to Maua, but then he said he couldn't. The coup was coming, he said. He couldn't be that far from his phone."

Lucia looked at her quietly. "Are you sure it's just the coup?"

Marina stopped crying. The summer breeze warming her back suddenly felt cold. "What do you mean?" she said.

"Well, he is the ambassador of the United States of America. Do you think he can really afford to be seen out in Rio with a call girl? Oh, I know you've retired. But there are going to be other people out there who knew you when. . . . "

"He says he loves me."

"Sure, but how many times has he taken you to the Ouro Verde restaurant for dinner? Or to the Copacabana Palace? Or even for tea at the Confeitaria Colombo? You know the answer. He can only take you to places where you won't be seen together, like Buzios. And now, with the coup about to happen, he can't even take you there."

"You mean he's ashamed of me?"

"Maybe. Or maybe he's just not willing to put his career at stake. He is a professional diplomat. That's enough crying for now, you'll make the ocean even saltier."

"Do you think he doesn't love me?"

"I don't think anything. Why don't you find out?"

"How?" Marina wailed.

"Give him a deadline."

"How? What kind of deadline?"

"Pick a date. Any date will do. And pick a fine restaurant in Copacabana where all the fancy gringos go. Like the Ouro Verde or the Copacabana Palace. Then tell him that you want to go there for dinner on the date you picked. And you tell him if he doesn't do it, you'll leave him the next day. And then you can come back to me."

Some of the old excitement reappeared in Marina's eyes, the tears gone for now. "What date should I choose?" she asked, ignoring Lucia's last offer. "How about the date the coup is supposed to happen?"

"I don't know," said Lucia. "When is that?"

"Probably April 2, or maybe the first."

"That sounds good," Lucia said. "And if he doesn't take you to dinner at the Copacabana Palace on April 2, it's all over between you."

"That's perfect, it's just perfect," Marina said. Her eyes were shining. "We'll have a wonderful dinner. And we'll drink a toast of champagne to you, Lucia!" She picked up her glass. "For now, we'll toast to ourselves," she said. She raised her glass to the sky.

"To good friends! To you, Lucia!"

Lucia looked longingly at Marina's gorgeous body, and smiled.

"To April 3," she said very softly, so Marina couldn't hear. "And our dinner together that night."

CHAPTER 22

Carter drove back to Marina's apartment in the Fusca. Marina should be back from Bangu, he thought. And this time, he swore to himself, he would not mention the coup, even though he would have to go back to the office tomorrow, although tomorrow was a Sunday. But for tonight, he would forget about the coup. They would make love as if they were in Buzios, or Bahia, or anywhere else without a radio or TV. That's what they would do after the coup was over. And that's what they would do tonight. He couldn't wait. He prayed she had come home.

She had. He could smell the garlic and the black beans and the pork as he climbed the stairs to her apartment. She rushed to embrace him at the door, wearing her yellow-and-green apron and nothing else, and kissed him, a long, warm, and gentle kiss. "I just couldn't stand being angry at you any more," she said. "I hoped so much you would be home for dinner so we could celebrate. And here you are!" He could feel himself growing hard already. "I've made you a *feijoada*," she said happily. "And a caipirinha with little sugar, just the way you like it. And for later on, I have a surprise! You're gonna like it!"

Carter slipped his hands down from her back to the cheeks of her perfect ass.

"It's no surprise," he said. "I know what it is, and let's not keep it for later, let's do it now."

Marina put on her pout.

"You men are all the same, all you ever think about is sex. I spent the whole afternoon cooking dinner for you, and before we make love, we're going to eat dinner in the nude. After that, you can eat me. And then, you'll get your surprise. So take off your clothes," she said, "right now!"

"Okay," Carter said.

The pout disappeared from Marina's lips.

"You're going to love it," she said.

He did. The *feijoada* was delicious: garlicky black beans, sausage, dried beef, a cut of pork he didn't recognize and chose not to ask. There was *farofa*, ground manioc root dried and gently toasted, sliced oranges, bitter greens, and, of course, lots of rice. She had bought imported beer and chilled it ice cold. For dessert, she had made *cocada preta*, one of his favorites, made of shredded coconut and sugar toasted in her toaster oven until it turned sticky dark brown. All in the nude.

The sex was fantastic, too. Just like it had been before their fight. Warmer somehow, but also even more exciting than it had been then. And all that, the wonderful meal, the delicious sex, all of that in Rio de Janeiro. God, he thought how many ambassadors had that?

He was almost asleep when Marina bit him gently on the ear. "Don't you want your surprise?"

"Sure," he said.

Marina smiled proudly.

"Well," she said, "the coup will happen on April 2."

"What?"

"I said the coup will happen April 2, or maybe the first."

Carter snapped upright on the bed.

"How do you know?"

"I just know."

"What does that mean, 'I just know'?"

"Well, someone told me. Someone who knows."

"How do you know he told you the truth?"

"I know." Marina didn't like Carter's cross-examination. "I thought you'd be happy," she said. There was a catch in her throat. "I did it for you."

"I am happy, sweetheart," Carter said. "It's just that it's really secret information. There's no way you could find out."

"I found out. The coup will start on April 2, or maybe the first," she said again.

Dear God, Carter thought, she does know, and that's too late. Brother Sam will probably have passed into Brazilian waters by then. And the Russians will have sunk it. Somehow Brother Sam had to be turned around before it reached Brazilian waters, or it had to arrive after the coup was over. After April 2. After that Brother Sam wouldn't be needed any more. After that, he might be able to persuade Washington to stop the flotilla before it entered Brazilian waters.

"Are you sure? April 2?"

"Yes, I'm sure. And I had to work very hard to find out." Marina burst into tears. "I found it out for you, Tony, only for you."

Carter gathered her up in his arms.

"I know you did, sweetheart," he said. "And I really appreciate it. Thank you, darling." He kissed her. "Only I wish that April 2 wasn't the date."

"You wish it was later?"

"No, I wish it was earlier."

They were almost asleep when he felt Marina nudge him.

"Are you awake?" she asked him a few moments later.

"Sort of. Why?"

"Because if the coup is going to happen by April 2, they won't need you any more after that. Isn't that right?"

"I don't know yet, darling."

Marina was starting to cry again. "Ever since I met you, Tony, I've played second violin to a coup that's not even yours. I'm not going to wait anymore. I love you so much," she said. "But I just can't stand it any more."

"I adore you."

"Yes," she said, "but not as much as you adore playing ambassador, and working on the coup. The coup is your mistress more than I am. It's your jealous lover, and I just can't compete."

"You are my lover, not the damn coup."

"I'm not a whore any more, Tony. I have only one lover, and that's you. But you can only have one lover, too. And that lover has to be me. I'm not going to compete any more with a damn coup. It's scheduled for no later than April 2. All right, I'll stay out of your way until April 2. If I'm not first by then, you and I will be finished, and you can do what you like with your coup."

"But darling," he said, "I'm the American ambassador. I can't promise. . . . "

She was up out of the bed now.

"I mean it, Tony. I mean it, April 2, and that's all! It's up to you! Who do you love most, me or your coup? You will have to decide."

She ran into the bathroom, slamming the door behind her.

CHAPTER 23

On Sunday mornings after coffee, Ambassador Sverdlov would sit on his veranda smoking a good Cuban cigar and reading last week's *Pravda* until at one o'clock he lay down on the sofa in his study and fell asleep. It was the best time of the week. Any interruptions were strictly forbidden, except when it was the red telephone on the coffee table.

It rang precisely at 2:00 p.m. He swore a heavy Russian oath and picked up the phone. There was the usual static, popping and squealing, which always accompanied the radio calls from Moscow. He could barely hear a voice shouting above the static.

"Comrade Sverdlov?"

"Yes."

"Just a moment. The premier will speak to you." Nikita Kruschev, premier of the government of the Soviet Union, was on the phone a moment later.

"Comrade Sverdlov," he shouted. The static had stopped and the premier's voice almost blew out his eardrums.

"I can hear you loud and clear, comrade. The connection is excellent now."

"Well, why didn't you say so?" the premier demanded. "The American task force is nearing Brazilian waters and moving south," Kruschev shouted. "They haven't stopped!"

"Yes, comrade," Sverdlov said.

"I am going to blow them out of the water! How often do they think they can rub my nose in dog shit? Once was enough, in Cuba, more than enough. And this is Brazil, not some piss-ass little island in the Caribbean!"

"Yes, comrade," Sverdlov said again. "Of course you are right, one hundred percent right!"

"That Goulag is a weakling, but at least he's our weakling. You must make sure nothing happens to him. The Americans shoot presidents they don't like."

"Goulart," Sverdlov said. "His name is Goulart." It was true, he thought. Carter wouldn't do that if it were up to him, but it probably wasn't. As far as he could tell the CIA was almost completely out of the embassy's control. He wondered whether his own KGB people worked the same way.

"I'll do my best, comrade," he said.

"You had better. If those ships don't stop by the time they reach Brazilian waters, they will go to the bottom of the sea!"

"If I may be so bold, Comrade Premier, might it be advisable to raise these issues with the American president? He is, after all, the commander in chief of the American armed forces."

"Johnson?" Kruschev was shouting again. "That cowboy? I am not about to call him. If he wants to talk, he can call me. Besides," he said, "there's nothing to talk about. The American ships must stop. That's it. There is nothing more to talk about."

"Talking never hurts," the ambassador said. There was a pause on the other end of the line. "Are you still there, comrade?"

"Yes, I'm still here," Kruschev said. "All right, if you want to talk, you can talk. Talk to their ambassador, talk to Johnson, talk to whoever you like, but remember, if the American flotilla goes one inch into Brazilian waters, that is the end of it. We will send it to the bottom of the sea!"

"Yes, Comrade Premier," Sverdlov said, but the line had already gone dead, and the static and squeals were back.

The envelope arrived at the Soviet embassy residence at about four o'clock marked simply "Ambassador Sverdlov." Sverdlov was surprised: He was not awaiting any documents. And why would they deliver anything to his house on a Sunday? He picked up his silver letter opener, and slit the envelope open. Inside were two photographs clipped together with a card that read simply "With compliments." Nothing to show who they were from.

The photographs were of two quite different people, separately coming out of a building on Siqueira Campos in the rain. Sverdlov knew them both: one was Carter, the other Marina. Just as beautiful as she was a couple of years ago, he thought, maybe more so. Was it possible that she was still working for his KGB people? Or for both sides? It looked like she was working for Carter now, although you never knew. Working in bed, he thought, with some envy. He should never have let her go.

It was a perfect setup for a little blackmail. The American ambassador and his call girl, coming out of the same building. If the premier's torpedoes didn't turn Brother Sam around, maybe the photos could. The issue wasn't up to Carter, though. Blackmail probably wouldn't work, but perhaps it was worth a try. But to what end?

The ambassador picked up the black phone on his desk. "Get me Ambassador Carter," he said to the switchboard operator. "Urgent."

Carter showed up at the Soviet residence in the Cadillac at 5:30 p.m. Not wise, he thought, but he hadn't been able to find a taxi, and Sverdlov's secretary had said it was urgent. Sverdlov's secretary was now showing him into one of the downstairs reception rooms. Sverdlov was there waiting.

"Anthony," he said warmly. "Come in, come in. Would you like a vodka, some whiskey, perhaps?"

Carter knew the Russian's vodka was excellent. "Thank you,

Ivan," he said. "Vodka would be fine." I wonder what he wants, he thought. At the Soviet residence, the vodka only flowed for a reason.

There was a fixed diplomatic protocol that defined the order of conversation. It began with the weather: too hot, they agreed. Then on to football: Sverdlov was for Flamengo, with its black and red uniforms. Carter rooted for Fluminense. The obligatory next subject was women. The Russian walked over to the sideboard and picked up the envelope.

"I have something to show you," he said.

Carter looked at the envelope. "I think I've seen it already," he said.

"I doubt that," said the Russian. "Go ahead, open it up."

Carter took the envelope and let the photos slide out. "Yes, Ivan," he said. "I've seen them—I even have a set. Nice, aren't they? They were delivered to the embassy by a fellow in a taxi. I didn't know they were sent by you."

"They weren't," Sverdlov said. "I don't know who—"

Carter cut him off. "You never know anything, Ivan. And, of course, you don't know who is trying to blackmail me, or why. What did you hope to achieve, Ivan? What do you want? The key to my liquor cabinet, perhaps? Or maybe the ignition key to our aircraft carrier?"

But the Russian wasn't listening. He had picked up the photo of Marina. "Ah, Marina," he sighed. "Isn't she magnificent? You are a very lucky man. . . . She used to work for us, you know."

Carter stared at him.

"Oh," the Russian continued, "there are so many ways we could blackmail you, Anthony. Marina is only one of them. But what would we blackmail you for? There's nothing you have that we want, except, as you said, the ignition key to your aircraft carrier, and you don't have it. You have to turn your task force around, Anthony, before it enters Brazilian waters. But we both want that. There's no need for blackmail."

You son of a bitch, Carter thought, you'd blackmail me in a

heartbeat if you thought you could get something useful out of me. But he said only, "You have to speak to your premier, Ivan."

"I did, earlier this afternoon. He knows where your flotilla is, and that it's moving south. Our submarines have told him that. He knows how many of your marines are hidden on board your *Forrestal*, and how many planes. Our intelligence has told him that. He is furious. If your task force passes into Brazilian waters, he will send it to the bottom of the sea. You cannot wait, Anthony. That task force will not reach Brazil. Either it turns around or we will sink it. Our submarines can do that and they will."

"Your premier must call my president," Carter said, "before he even thinks of anything like that. It could mean the end of the world as we know it."

"He won't. He wants Mr. Johnson to call *him*. You have to make him do that."

"I can try," Carter said, though he knew his chances were close to zero. Well, he could try.

"Your vodka's getting warm," the Russian said. He raised his glass. "*Nasdrovia*," he said. "Good luck."

The pictures were still on Sverdlov's desk when Carter left. What use would they be in Brazil? Blackmail? The Brazilians would only applaud Carter's good taste in women. But the Americans were different, more puritanical. The photos just might be useful there some day. He buzzed his secretary.

"Send these by pouch to Ambassador Michelaikov in Washington," he said. "Tell him I'll call later to explain."

In his mind's eye, Carter could imagine the *Forrestal* steaming into Guanabara Bay, with perhaps fifty aircraft aboard and some 2,000 troops below decks, then heading into the harbor just around the corner from his view. The Russian submarines could hardly have missed the world's largest aircraft carrier steaming down the Atlantic coast toward Rio de Janeiro. But how in hell had the Russians found out about the troops and the aircraft below her decks? How could Krushchev know when he, the American ambassador, did not? Someone on the American side was feeding that information to the Soviets, but there was no one in Rio who knew. The spy had to be in Washington, or on the *Forrestal* itself.

The red light flashed on his telephone. "I have Washington," the switchboard operator said. "It's Mr. Mahon."

Shit, Carter said to himself. Mahon was not one of his favorites. "Carter," Mahon's voice rasped into the phone, "What's the problem?"

"I need to speak with the president," he said.

"You can speak with me," the voice said.

"No," Carter said. "I need to speak with the president."

"About what?"

"I'll explain that to him."

"Look, goddamn it, if you're talking about Brother Sam, you talk to me. You were ordered to keep out of it."

"Up yours!"

"I'll have your ass, Tony," Mahon said. "I'll have your fucking ass." There was a click and a long silence. The red light on the phone remained on though, and Carter knew that Mahon had only put him on hold. I wonder who I get next, he thought.

A deep, loud voice with a pronounced Texas twang came booming over the line. "Tony," the president exclaimed, "Where the hell are you, boy? We're having one helluva barbecue out here. Whyn't you get on a plane and get yourself up here? You can bring that gorgeous piece of ass of yours up with you, if you want."

God, Carter thought, how does he know about Marina? "Thanks, Mr. President," he said. "But I think I'm needed here just now."

"Where's that?"

"I'm in Rio de Janeiro, sir."

"Nice beaches, they tell me," the president said. "Lotsa nice pussy."

"Mr. President, we may be on the verge of a terrible disaster here, sir."

"Yeah? What's that?" The president's voice had suddenly gone harder.

"Brother Sam," Carter said. "The Soviet ambassador here has told me that Premier Khrushchev has directed his submarines to sink the *Forrestal* if it passes into Brazilian waters. It's important that you call Premier Khrushchev right away, sir. There is no need for this confrontation. The Brazilian military doesn't need Brother Sam. It can successfully carry out its revolution without us."

"You want me to call that little turd?"

"Yes, sir."

"Listen, Tony. If that little shit wants to talk, he can call me. Or better, he can call Mahon. He may be a prick, but he's in charge of this operation. I understand State has ordered you to keep out of it. I think that's best, Tony. You just keep out of it."

The red light on Carter's phone went out. The president had hung up.

Ambassador Sverdlov answered the phone at his residence personally. He was plainly annoyed. "Well," he asked, "did you get him?"

"Yes," Carter said.

"And?"

"He's just as stubborn as your premier. He'd probably take the call if your premier called him, but he isn't about to initiate the call himself. He's too proud for that. He has delegated the whole problem to an assistant secretary of state."

Sverdlov grunted. "You mean Mahon? What do you call him? We call him a small penis."

Carter grinned. "Not 'small penis,' Ivan, 'little prick' is what we say." He laughed. "I needed that, Ivan," he said. "Thank you."

He could hear Sverdlov chuckling on the other end of the line. "What else?" the Russian asked.

"He ordered me again to keep out of it."

There was a long silence. "You'd better not," the Russian said. "There is no one else. There is nothing I can do. Your flotilla has got to stop. It has to turn around. You have to make that happen."

"There's no way I can do that, Ivan. I'm not the commander in chief, the president is. And unless he orders it to stop, the flotilla will continue south until it reaches Rio de Janeiro or until it is sunk by your submarines. They have to pull back. Only your government can turn your subs around. You have to make that happen, Ivan."

"There's no way I can make that happen either."

There was another long silence. "We'll just have to do the best we can," Carter said. "But I don't know what that could be."

"Yes," said the Russian. He hung up.

CHAPTER 24

Harry drove into the parking lot behind the Parque Guinle Apartments a little after nine thirty on Monday morning. The customs hearing was scheduled to begin at 9:30 and would run all day. He had all the time in the world for the "dress rehearsal." By noon he would know just how and where the best sight lines were between Thornton's apartment and the road where Jango's limousine would pass. He would know the locks and the alarms, if there were any. He would be all ready once the date was fixed.

Harry got out of the car carrying a leather briefcase, and walked nonchalantly to the building. He had seen no doorman or guards when he drove up, but he nonetheless checked carefully for any cameras near the back door. There were none.

The inside of the building was deserted. Harry ignored the elevator and ducked through the adjoining door marked Exit. He climbed the stairs to the sixth floor, panting heavily by the time he arrived. Shit, he thought, this intelligence business is murder. I've got to get in shape.

Getting into Thornton's apartment was duck soup. Picking the dead bolt lock took Harry less than a minute. Then he took a plastic queen of spades from his pocket, slipped it into the edge of the door, and pushed gently. The door lock clicked and the door swung open. Harry stepped inside and quietly closed the door.

It was a sunny apartment, furnished with Swedish modern style furniture provided by the embassy. An entry hall led into the living room. Another hall on the right led to the bedroom, bathroom, and the kitchen. Harry quickly checked them out. Empty.

Across the front of the living room was a line of low windows looking south over the top of Parque Guinle onto the Laranjeiras Palace on the other side. The road from the bottom of the park at the Rua das Laranjeiras ran in front of the buildings, then snaked its way up the hill and across to the palace at the top of the park. There were at least a dozen clean shots from the apartment at any car that came down the hill from the palace to the Rua das Laranjeiras. There was one more road that ran down from the back of the palace to the Rua das Flores behind the hill. The president might take that road. But it would be simple for Oscar to get that road closed off on April 1. Jango would have no way to leave the palace without driving down the road in front of the building and in front of the crosshairs in Harry's Uzi. It was perfect, absolutely perfect.

Harry opened his briefcase and pulled out the red felt package inside. He could feel the parts of the disassembled gun in its custom-fitted bag. The feel of the hard steel inside its soft container always gave him a thrill, and he could feel himself getting hard inside his pants.

Harry took the rifle out of the bag and expertly fitted it together. It was his most cherished possession.

The windows at the front of the room were designed to open by sliding sideways. Since it was the end of summer, and the air-conditioning had been on nonstop, they had not been open for months. After some struggle, Harry managed to open one of them. He reached again into his briefcase and pulled out a short steel tri-pod. It had a small cradle device on the top. Harry pulled out the legs so that the cradle was about two feet above the windowsill. Then he lay down on the floor, set the barrel of the gun into the cradle, and looked through the view finder at the road where it emerged from behind the trees at the top of the hill. He didn't need the tripod, but he might as well make absolutely certain. Perfect, he thought again. He could shoot an orange or a lemon in half from there. Blowing off the president's head was easy. And with the right ammunition, they would never know where the shot had come from.

He was still musing about the ease of the job when he heard a key turn in the kitchen door of the apartment and the door open. "Shit," he breathed. He glanced at his watch. It was 12:15. The fucking idiots at customs must have taken a break for lunch. He quickly rolled into the entry hall where he could not be seen from the hall leading from the kitchen. He could hear the steps coming down the hall and into the living room. He could see Thornton from the back now, staring at the tripod and the gun. "What the hell?" Thornton exclaimed.

Harry was on his feet before Thornton could turn around. He grasped hard on both sides of Thornton's head, his hands around his ears, and violently twisted his head to the right. At the same time, he thrust his right leg between Thornton's legs and shoved him hard to the left. Harry heard the satisfying crack of Thornton's breaking neck as he fell to the floor. Harry looked down at his victim. "I'm sorry," he said. "You didn't leave me much choice."

"You son of a bitch!" Thornton whispered.

"Hold still," Harry said, although he knew that Thornton was paralyzed. He walked over to the open window and looked down at the ground five stories below. There was a two-meter-wide concrete apron that ran all around the building. A broad hedge of tropical plants hid the apron from the road.

Harry carefully took the rifle from the top of the tripod, collapsed its legs, and put it into the briefcase. Then he lovingly disassembled the gun and placed the pieces in the red felt bag. He put the bag in the briefcase as well.

"Well, I guess that's it," Harry said. He walked slowly over to Thornton, took hold of his ankles, and dragged him to the window. It took some effort for him to turn Thornton around so his head was near the open window, and then to roll him onto his stomach. "I'm sorry, my friend," Harry said. "It's all in the interests of our country."

It was even harder for Harry to drag Thornton's crumpled body up onto the windowsill so that the upper part of his body hung out the window over the sill. Harry looked out across the park. It was empty except for two children and a nanny under the trees in the far corner of the park. The nanny was facing the opposite direction.

"Good bye, my friend," Harry said. "This won't hurt long."

"You shit!" Thornton gasped.

Harry picked up Thornton's ankles and held them above his head. Thornton's body slid out the window. Harry could hear his neck break again as it hit the concrete. He looked down out of the window. Thornton's body lay well hidden by the hedge.

"You do nice work," Harry said to himself. Actually, it's not very nice, he thought, but sometimes these things had to be done, in the interests of his country. He closed the window and went quietly out the front door. He left the dead bolt unlocked.

The old Cadillac drove slowly up the road through Guinle Park to the presidential palace and stopped at the ceremonial entrance. An office boy stood waiting by the door. "The president will see you shortly," the boy said in his most important-sounding voice.

"*Beleza,*" Carter said. "Beautiful." The boy looked annoyed, but said nothing. Carter was in Goulart's private office five minutes later.

"Mr. Ambassador," the president said. "What can I do for you?"

"It's a nice day," Carter said.

"Yes," Goulart said, "but they say it may rain."

"Well," Carter said, "that's possible. Let's have a look at the clouds." He motioned toward the balcony.

"Good idea," the president said. As soon as they were outside, he turned to Carter. "All right, Anthony," he said. "What have you brought me? Another ultimatum?"

"No," Carter said. "I'm afraid it's the same one. Only I didn't give you all of it last time. And I can't give you all of it now. It's classified. But I am going to give you the last paragraph even if it is: It contains the message I am supposed to give you." Carter handed Goulart a small piece of paper. "Remember, Jango, I didn't write this. It comes from Washington."

Goulart took the paper, read it, then read it again out loud.

"You may assure the president that if he complies with our request, we will see to it that he is protected against any risk to his person or to his family which might otherwise occur."

"So, what does it mean?" he asked softly.

"Well," Carter said, "I can't really say. But it could mean that they will try to assassinate both you and your family unless you knuckle under."

"Knuckle under?"

"Comply with their ultimatum."

"Why didn't you tell me this in our last meeting?"

"Because I couldn't do it, Jango. I couldn't threaten the president of Brazil that the United States might kill you and your family unless you did as you were told. That just wasn't in me. And it still isn't."

The president gazed at him. "And now?" he finally said.

"Now," said Carter, "I'm going to get you out of here before the CIA does. But I'm going to get you out alive."

"And how do you propose to do that?"

"I don't know," Carter said, "but we're going to do it."

"When?"

"I'll let you know. Probably April 1."

"Why April 1?"

"Because the coup is likely to happen April 2, so the CIA will probably schedule your execution no later than April 1, that's our April Fools' Day. The Agency has a macabre sense of humor. I want to get you out of here before that. Besides, they prefer to kill presidents just before a coup. That way there's no time for the people to get agitated before the coup actually happens."

"And how do you know when the coup is going to happen?"

Carter grinned. "My girlfriend told me," he said.

Goulart didn't think that was funny. "The CIA is your girlfriend, Anthony?" he asked.

"Mr. President," Carter said, "I have no idea what the CIA is doing. I don't really know what their plans are. In fact, I'm not even sure who their people in Brazil are. Sometimes they seem to know more than I do. The CIA is almost a government of its own. But my best information is April 1 or 2."

"Come inside," Goulart said. He walked to the middle of the room. Carter followed him in.

"Mr. Ambassador," Goulart said, "I thank you for your visit. But the government of Brazil cannot accept any ultimatum or threats of any kind, whether by the United States or any other power. We are an independent republic and will not tolerate any interference in our internal affairs or any threats to our elected officials. Now, if you will forgive me, I have important matters to attend to." He turned and strode out of the room.

CHAPTER 25

Although Carter arrived at the embassy at nine o'clock, early for him, the Soviet ambassador apparently had gotten up even earlier.

"Ambassador Sverdlov called at eight o'clock," Joannie told him, "right after I got in. His secretary asked me to let her know as soon as you arrived, and the ambassador will pick you up in front of the Teatro Municipal."

The Teatro Municipal was the jewel of downtown Rio de Janeiro. Several years ago, Carter, Sverdlov, and their wives had actually gone together to a concert performance of *Pique Dame* by a visiting Russian opera company. It was, Carter recalled, an entirely pleasant evening. He doubted his conversation with Sverdlov this morning would be as agreeable.

Sverdlov's limousine, an aging black GAZ 13 Chaika, ground around the corner and stopped at the front steps of the theater. Carter was there waiting.

"What's this, Ivan?" he asked. "What happened to our taxi arrangement?"

"Get in," Sverdlov said. "Yes, of course this car is bugged. And I'm going to record every word we say. I'll let you have a copy of the tape, if you like. This time, if your government chooses to lie to us again later on, it won't be able to deny what was said today. We'll have it on tape for the whole world to hear. We are tired of your lies."

"We don't lie, Ivan." Carter said with a straight face.

The Russian snorted. "Well, that's news," he said.

The cars behind them were honking impatiently. Carter stepped into the car and closed the door. Sverdlov said something to the driver in Russian, and the car sped off down Avenida Rio Branco, ignoring the traffic lights, and onto the Atero Parkway, which ran along the side of Guanabara Bay, linking downtown Rio with Copacabana, fifteen kilometers away. There, the car turned right onto Avenida Atlantica, passed in front of the Copacabana Palace Hotel, crossed Rua Siqueira Campos, and continued down the beach to the army fort and the Bar Atlantico at Posto 6. There, the car turned right again and passed a short stretch of apartment buildings before the road emerged onto the Ipanema beach.

The entire trip, the Russian sat staring grimly ahead in silence. Well, Carter thought, he'll speak when we get to their safe house in Leblon. But the car didn't turn in at Rua Rita Ludolf. Rather, at the end of the beach, the driver bore left onto a dirt road marked by a small sign that read Avenida Niemeyer. Carter knew that road. Marina and he had been there together. The road was carved into a cliff at the base of Dois Irmaos. Kind of appropriate, Carter thought. Here they were, the ambassadors of the two superpowers of the world, either one of which had more than enough atomic power to blow the world to smithereens. In a way, they were indeed two brothers.

He looked down over the edge of the road at the waves crashing on the rocks some sixty feet below. And, like two brothers, he thought, one may try to murder the other and destroy them both. It had happened before.

"You've read too much Shakespeare," Carter said to himself.

"What?" Sverdlov said.

"Oh, never mind."

The road ended at a white sand beach, deserted except for a small church and a primitive wooden structure with a Coca-Cola sign. Sverdlov motioned for the driver to turn the car to face the sea. He turned to Carter.

"Your flotilla is off Fortaleza," he said, "heading south. Unless it changes course, it will enter Brazilian waters at Recife or at the latest at Salvador. And that carrier, it's the *Forrestal*, right? She's your largest carrier."

"It is?" said Carter.

"Don't bullshit me, Anthony. How many planes are on that carrier? And how many troops?"

"I don't know, Ivan," he said, "and I couldn't tell you, even if I did."

"Lies, lies, lies," Sverdlov shouted. "You make believe you don't know. Of course you know. You take me for a fool! You are the ambassador for the United States. Of course you know. And I am not a fool!"

"I know you're not a fool, Ivan. But I really don't know. I have been ordered by Washington to stay out of this, that it's being handled there. I am not even supposed to know that the operation exists, let alone know what or where our ships are or what's on them. You've been in the diplomatic service for a long time, Ivan. You've been an ambassador for twenty years. Has the Kremlin never done something similar to you? Your government will just have to speak with Washington."

"Washington!" the Russian exploded. "Washington is a city. It doesn't speak. Then we are told to speak to 'desk.' A desk is a piece of furniture that some fools sit on. It doesn't speak either. So we are referred to secretary. I have secretary, you have secretary, we all have secretary, only some make shorthand better than others. No, no, they say, not that kind of secretary, big important secretaries like secretary of state or secretary of defense. But these secretaries tell us nothing except that they have no power to speak anything without approval of president. And your president." Sverdlov paused for breath. "Your president is on vacation in his rancho in Texas. All the time!

"We have done a little research," Sverdlov continued, "and under your laws, you are the representative of your president here in Brazil, his emissary. You report directly to him. You are here in Rio de Janeiro, and even if you lie, I can see your face. I can speak directly to you, not to some secretary. And that is what I will continue to do."

"I don't really report to the president," Carter protested, "I report to the—"

Sverdlov held up his hand. "We can read your law as well as you can," he said. "You have authority. You are head of country team and you report to your president." He opened the car door and walked down to the sea, beckoning for Carter to follow.

"I'm sorry, Anthony," he said when he arrived at the water. "You know the car is bugged. I had to say all that to cover my rectum, as you Americans say. There are some in the Kremlin who are not too fond of me . . . " he paused. "You might not realize, Anthony, why Brother Sam is so important. But missile crisis between our premier and Mr. Kennedy happened only two years ago. There are still a lot of important people in Kremlin and in the armed forces who are very upset that we back down in Cuba. If we were to back down again in Brazil, our premier and this government might well fall and I have no idea what would come next. You must know all this already, but situation in Moscow has become even more unstable since missiles and Cuba.

"Your aircraft carrier and your flotilla made a serious mistake," Sverdlov continued. "They passed less than 200 miles from the Cuban coast on their way to Brazil. Cuba claims 200-nautical-mile territorial limit, and our submarines patrol those waters for them. We could hardly miss your flotilla going by. Our submarines have, of course, remained close to it since then. We know precisely where they are and we will continue to know. We can sink your carrier whenever we choose."

Sverdlov paused. "Our submarines are armed with nuclear warheads, Anthony. You know that. I have been instructed to tell you again that your flotilla may not proceed into Brazilian waters. Doing so will be considered by Soviet Union to be a hostile act and treated as such."

Carter watched a seagull drop into the surf and pull out a gleaming silver fish. "What does that mean?" he asked.

"Your guess is as good as mine," the Russian said, "but it surely is not pleasant." He paused. "Certainly the end of your carrier," he said, "and the troops and planes on board. Probably nuclear war."

The ride back to Rio passed again in silence. Although their countries were enemies, Carter thought he felt some kind of bond developing between him and the large, bearded Russian diplomat sitting taciturn next to him. The car stopped at the side door of the American embassy. Carter got out and reached over to shake the Russian's hand. "We can't let it happen, Ivan," he said.

The Russian nodded silently.

CHAPTER 26

The *Forrestal* was the largest aircraft carrier in the world. Of course there were planes. Why wouldn't there be troops as well? Did that mean the United States was planning to actually invade Brazil if the coup failed? And how did Sverdlov know that the carrier was the *Forrestal?* How did he know about the troops?

He buzzed the intercom for Joannie.

"Good morning, Mr. Ambassador," her voice chirped over the intercom. "I see you sneaked in the back way. Coffee?"

"Yes, please."

She was in his office a moment later bearing coffee, water, the *Jornal do Brasil,* and the English-language *Brazil Herald.* "Must have been a nice visit with Ambassador Sverdlov. You were gone more than two hours."

"No such thing as a nice visit with Ambassador Sverdlov," he said. "It was OK. Call General Werner for me, will you, Joannie? Ask him to come over as soon as he can. Oh, and send out for a couple of grilled ham and cheese sandwiches for me, will you? You know, those wonderful *mixto quentes* you got me last week? And two Cokes, please. I'm having lunch at my desk."

For a moment, Carter played with the idea of not reporting his conversation with Sverdlov to Washington. They wouldn't pay any attention to his report anyway. They would merely chastise him again for even speaking with Sverdlov. Hopefully, they were speaking to the Kremlin directly. Nonetheless, he had better send something to Washington . . . if only to cover his rectum, as the Russian had said. He turned to the typewriter next to his desk.

TOP SECRET
For SecState

*I was asked by Soviet Ambassador Sverdlov to meet with him
this morning to discuss the present location of Brother Sam
ships and what they had aboard. I explained that I was not in
the loop on this subject and had no information on the matter.
I repeated that any questions or comments relating to this matter
should be addressed solely to Washington.*

*Nevertheless, he insisted on informing me that the flotilla was being
tracked by Soviet submarines bearing nuclear warheads and it
was known by his government to be presently located off Fortaleza
on the north coast of Brazil. He stated that his government would
not permit a repeat of the humiliation they suffered two years ago
in Cuba, and warned of the risk of nuclear war if the flotilla pro-
ceeded into Brazilian waters. He appeared to be very concerned.*

—Carter

Well, he thought to himself, that will either send them into a frenzy or it won't. It should. But it probably won't. He buzzed Joannie again.

"They're not here yet, chief. Neither the sandwiches nor General Werner."

"That's okay," he said. "I've got a cable for you to type, if you would, please."

"Yes, sir," she said.

General Werner arrived five minutes later. "I'm sorry I'm late, sir. I was. . . . "

Carter cut him off. "It's fine," he said. He walked around his desk and sat down in his favorite brown leather easy chair.

"Sit down, Otto," he said, waving Werner onto the sofa.

"Well," he said, once Werner had settled in, "where's the *Forrestal* now?"

Werner looked startled. "The *Forrestal*? I don't know, sir," he said. "Somewhere off the north coast of Brazil, I suppose."

"Don't give me that bullshit, Otto. It's off Fortaleza, and you know damn well where it is. And what's its ETA in Rio?"

Werner remained silent.

"I don't know that, sir," he finally said. "I really don't."

"Well, find that out. And while we're at it, how many fighter planes are there on board the carrier? And how many choppers?"

"I don't know," Werner said again.

"Well, you'd better find that out, too." Carter snapped. "And how many troops?"

"I'm really sorry, Tony, but I'm afraid I don't have any information on any of that. As far as I know, there probably aren't any."

"I'm sorry, but I don't believe that, Otto. You either know or you have access to that information. I want those figures, not as far as you know, or how many there 'probably' are, but how many aircraft and how many troops there are actually there aboard that carrier, and on the destroyers."

Werner had turned white. Carter could see his bad leg trembling where the stump of his leg met the nickel of his prosthesis.

"That's classified information, sir," he said.

Carter could feel the blood pumping in his head as he stood up. Werner struggled to get to his feet as well.

"Sit down, Otto," Carter said, "and stay there." Werner slumped back onto the sofa.

"Now listen up, Otto, and listen good, as they say in your service.

As long as I am ambassador, I am the head of the country team. That means that everyone in this embassy from the janitor to the spooks reports to me, and that includes you. You know all that. And you know damn well that I am cleared for Top Secret, so classification is irrelevant. There is no information that may be kept secret from me by you or the CIA or anyone else. None. Have you got that straight?"

Werner nodded his head.

"So, Otto, please get that information to me by close of business today, without fail. I'm sure you can do that."

Werner struggled up out of the couch.

"Sit down, Otto," Carter said again. "I have something else to show you." He pulled Washington's cable about Operation Brother Sam out of the open safe behind him and handed it to Werner. Werner read the cable in silence. "Read the last paragraph again," Carter said, "read it aloud."

"We are, in fact, somewhat concerned that existence of Brother Sam has become known to embassy." Werner read. "Please report immediately the source of your information."

"I'll have to answer that," said Carter. "What do you want me to tell them?"

"I wasn't supposed to tell you about Brother Sam," Werner said softly. "It was a mistake."

"I know. I remember."

"I could get into a good deal of trouble for that."

"That's why I asked what you want me to do. But it's hard to lie to the secretary when he asks me a direct question like that. He is my boss, after all."

"Maybe you don't really need to answer right away?"

"I don't know," Carter said. "You'd better think about it while you get that information I asked you for." He turned to the sandwiches still wrapped on his desk. "Now, how about some lunch, Otto?"

"No, thank you," Werner said. He stood up and limped hurriedly out of the room.

Werner sat down at his typewriter the moment he arrived at his office.
He addressed the cable to McCone and classified it "TOP SECRET,
for your eyes only. DO NOT DISTRIBUTE OUTSIDE AGENCY."

*1. AMB has obtained knowledge from sources unknown to me of
the existence of Operation Brother Sam, and is now insisting
on further details. He is aware that the* Forrestal *is part of
the flotilla. I have been ordered to deliver to him by COB today
detailed information on the number of aircraft (including helicopters) and troops on board, and the flotilla's present location and
ETA at Rio.*

*2. In my judgment, it would be inadvisable to refuse AMB's order
in its entirety. Carter is no fool. He is head of the country team
with top-secret clearance and has every right to access this information. Refusal to provide it could well blow my cover.*

*3. This said, I see no reason why all information provided needs
to be entirely accurate. Carter is extremely upset by Brother
Sam and the fact that he was not consulted on the operation in
advance. He may yet seek some way to stop it. However, the
smaller he believes Brother Sam's muscle to be, the less likely
that he will feel it necessary to get in the way. For these reasons,
I intend to provide him later today with data regarding the
number of troops and aircraft on board the* Forrestal *that are
only twenty to thirty percent of the accurate figures. Obviously,
Admiral Whitcroft will have to be informed.*

*4. I do not believe, however, it would be wise to provide Carter
with an inaccurate date for the ETA of Brother Sam in Rio
de Janeiro. The hull speed of the* Forrestal *is readily available information. Unlike the troop and aircraft figures, the
time required for the task force to arrive in Rio can be quite
easily calculated once her present location is known. I can,
however, truthfully tell him that for the moment I do not*

know its position. Until Ambassador Carter has this informa-
tion, its ETA Rio cannot be accurately predicted, making his
interference extremely difficult. Admiral Whitcroft should be
instructed not to release information regarding task force loca-
tion under any circumstances.

5. *It is apparent from the facts above that Carter has a source of*
information regarding Brother Sam in addition to Washington
or myself. To protect his actual source, he may even claim that he
obtained the information from me. That is obviously untrue.

6. *I am concerned that Carter may be aware of Plan B as well,*
and may attempt to block it, notwithstanding its approval at
highest level USG. It must be remembered that AMB and
Goulart are personal friends. It is not impossible that if AMB
is or becomes aware of Plan B, he would warn president or even
attempt to thwart the plan's execution.

7. *As you know, AMB has been called to Washington for "imme-*
diate consultation" so that he will be out of the way here. (I am
prepared to take over as necessary.) Thus far there is no indica-
tion that he will comply. It may become necessary to activate
contingency plan that you and I discussed. General C. is willing
to act if required.

8. *In addition, I am forwarding to Langley by pouch some photo-*
graphic materials, which you may find interesting.

9. *I have requested an appointment with Marshal Braga, and will*
report on results after we meet.

Please call me on a secure line if you should wish further details.

General Werner read through the draft. It was a good cable, he
thought. It would go a little hard on Tony, but it would protect his
own skin. Besides, Tony must know where his risks came from: not the
Brazilian government, but from his own.

Werner stood up and limped down the hall to his cable room. He dismissed the duty officer and sat down to type the cable himself. This one was too important to let even the cable operator see it. He pressed the send button, then walked back to his office and picked up the phone.

"Get me Marshal Braga," he said to his adjutant. "Tell him it's urgent."

CHAPTER 27

Marshal Antonio Alberto Braga Neto, chief of staff of the Brazilian Army, sat at his desk on the sixth floor of the War Ministry, three blocks from Maua Square. The marshal stood five foot four in his stocking feet. He had screwed his desk chair as high as it would go so that he could peer over the windowsill, just barely, and see the statue of the Duque de Caixias near the entrance to the patio, which surrounded the Ministry six floors below. There were two tanks in the patio, which he had ordered moved there yesterday, and several unmanned machine gun emplacements. It was evening and the towers that capped the building cast their shadows past Maua Square, almost to the bay. It was his favorite time of day.

There were only two pieces of paper on top of his desk. One was the *Jornal of Brasil* of that morning, the other was a writing of his own. Almost the entire first page of the *Jornal of Brasil* was about the huge rally held the night before in front of the Central do Brasil train station, practically next to the Ministry of War. President Joao Goulart had announced his intention to carry out basic reforms of property rights in Brazil. From his office the marshal had heard the roar of the crowd and seen the red flags with hammer and sickle waving. The paper told him Jango had signed two decrees, one expropriating land along federal highways to give to the peasants, the other nationalizing the private petroleum refineries. Both had been objectives of the Communist Party for a long time. At the end of the rally the Minister of War, General Dantas Castro, had climbed up onto the speaker's platform and had given Jango a warm hug. Luiz Carlos Prestes, chairman of the Communist Party of Brazil, had done the same.

The marshal could stand no more of it. He set the newspaper down on his desk. The Communists were driving the country into bankruptcy. The inflation rate was going to reach 150 percent in 1964. The per-capita income had actually dropped for the first time since the end of the Second World War. Deficit spending by the government had reached an all time high. Maybe it was not all Jango's fault. But the Communists were using him to further their own objectives and he didn't have the strength to resist. The military would have to remove him from the presidency if Brazil was to be saved. There was no other choice.

The problem was how. Jango's minister of war had skillfully maneuvered Braga and his allies into positions of little or no importance, and entrusted the keys of power to officers loyal to Jango. For the second time that morning, the marshal stared down at the other paper on his desk. On it he had written a list of the important officers in the Brazilian armed forces. Each name was marked with No, Yes, or a question mark. No were those who supported Jango, Yes were those he could count on to work with him on Jango's overthrow. The question marks were those still up in the air. He read the list again.

> Dantas Castro .... No
> Ribeira .... No
> Oromar Verde .... No
> Duarte .... No
> Assis Brasil .... Yes
> Pinto Pequeno .... No
> Cardoso .... No
> Teixeira .... No

Castelo Verde .... Yes
Cordeiro Farias .... No
Ernesto Friseh .... Yes
Golbery .... Yes
Medici .... Yes
Ademar de Queiroz .... Yes
Barros .... ?
Guedes .... ?
Azevedo .... ?
Costa .... ?
Cordel .... ?

Eight for Jango, six against him, four undecided . . . and General
Cordel, the commanding officer of the Third Army in Sao Paulo.
Cordel was respected by every general in Brazil. His support was criti-
cal. So far, he was wavering, but still on Jango's side.

Marshal Braga picked up the paper and sighed. There were just
too many names marked No.

He did not want to get the Americans involved. He did not want
it when General Werner had mentioned the idea several months ago
and he did not want it now. He definitely did not want the gringos to
invade. That would unite the whole country behind Jango, including
the entire officer corps.

And yet, perhaps if the gringos stepped in, the list might not be as
important. They certainly were anxious to be a part of it. Operation
Brother Sam hadn't been Braga's idea. At first he had turned down
the suggestion when General Werner had made it three weeks ago. He
didn't need it, he thought then. The army could do the job without
the Americans. And the political fallout was likely to be horrendous
if Brother Sam were to become known. If anything, it would probably
push Cordel permanently into Jango's camp.

But he had concluded, after listening to Werner, that it might be
good to have Brother Sam secretly standing by, ready to jump in if it

was needed. In some circumstances, aerial bombardment of Jango's troops might be very helpful. So would having some American troops at his side. But was it wise to invite the Americans into Brazil? They might never leave.

"What would Your Excellency do?" Marshal Braga said out loud to the statute of the Duque de Caixias in the patio six stories below.

His phone rang, jolting the marshal out of his thoughts.

"General Werner is here," his adjutant said.

"You're sure it's not the Duque de Caixias?"

"What?"

"Oh, never mind. Send General Werner in."

Werner always felt a little ridiculous when he stood next to Braga. Werner was some seventeen inches taller than the marshal, and maybe double his weight.

"Antonio," he said, "thank you for receiving me on such short notice."

"It's always a pleasure to see you," Braga said.

They both knew this wasn't always true, but today the marshal was indeed happy to see him. "What can I do for you?" he asked.

"Well," Werner said, "I need your help. The ambassador knows about Brother Sam." The marshal nodded. "We don't know the date you have planned for the coup. It would be very helpful to know. Of course, we would want to make sure to coordinate the date Brother Sam arrives in Rio with the date the coup will occur. I'm sure you will want to have your cards stacked up and ready when the coup starts."

The marshal was totally lost. "What cards, Otto? Why are they stacked up?"

Werner laughed. "I'm sorry, Antonio. Figure of speech. I only meant you will want to have all your troops, your aircraft, all your backstop—I mean, backup—in place when the shooting starts."

"We hope there will be no shooting, Otto. We expect to resolve things by phone. That's the Brazilian way."

"I know, Antonio, but what if you can't? That's when you may want our troops, our planes, our oil, all under your own command, your control."

"How can I be sure of that," the marshal said. "Your country is going to turn over control of its troops and aircraft to the command of a Brazilian marshal? Come, Otto, you know that won't happen."

"Well," said Werner lamely, "indirectly."

"All right, Otto, all right. If your country is so anxious to participate. If we need your help, I will let you know. But there are a few conditions.

"First, you and your government must understand and agree that this is our fight. You don't come in unless and until we ask you in."

"Okay," Werner said. "Of course, you know I can't commit the US government to anything. Only the president can do that. But I'm sure he'll agree."

"All right, but you'll have to get his agreement before we can move ahead. Otherwise, no deal."

"Okay, Antonio," Werner said. "I'll let you know. What's next?"

"Second, the existence of Brother Sam is to be and remain completely secret, unless and until I call for your help. The only one who will know about Brother Sam is you and me and, apparently, the ambassador, and you will take instructions only from me. You will neither inform nor deal with anyone else, unless authorized by me."

"Done," Werner said.

"Third, there will be a major foreign aid program for Brazil under the Alliance for Progress if the coup is successful. It will involve at least half a billion dollars a year in long-term loans and grants."

"I'm afraid I can't do that one, Antonio. Foreign aid funds are appropriated by the US Congress. We can't commit money that hasn't been appropriated."

The marshal glared across his desk. "Don't give me legalisms, Otto. Your government can find half a billion dollars a year somewhere if it wants to."

No point in arguing, Werner thought. The State Department legal advisor would never agree, but at this stage he'd rather fight with him than with Braga. Anyway, the Bureau of Inter-American Affairs at State wasn't that squeamish about what the law was.

"Okay, Antonio," he said. "But again, the president will have to approve."

"I know," said the marshal. "I know."

"So, what's number four?" Somehow, Werner knew that number four would be the most difficult.

Braga turned and stared out the window at the gathering dusk. He could still see the statue of the Duque de Caixias on his horse far below. He turned his chair back around to face Werner. "Your CIA seems to like to assassinate foreign presidents if your government doesn't like them," he said. "That is not going to happen here, Otto. We are a civilized country. Jango will not be assassinated, either by you or by us. We will see that he leaves the country and that he doesn't come back. But he will not be assassinated. He is a good man who has gone politically astray and must be removed from office. But he is not to be killed. Do I make myself clear?"

Werner had been afraid this was coming. Personally he had opposed Plan B. But in the end, the Agency and Assistant Secretary Mahon had persuaded the president to approve the plan. He could not commit the United States to just the opposite course from the one the president had approved.

"Have I made myself clear?" the marshal said again.

"Very clear," Werner said.

"All right," Braga said. "When can I expect to have your president's commitment on these points?"

"I don't know," Werner said. "He's on vacation in Texas, and in any case, you have to go through a lot of bureaucracy before you get to him." He stopped. "It would help if we knew the date you expect the coup to happen."

"I don't know that yet," Braga said. "We don't have all our

people lined up yet, all our geese in a row, as you say. When will Brother Sam arrive in Rio?"

Werner hesitated. "I'm not sure, he said. "It depends on the weather, the wind, the currents, and the displacement of the ship. . . . " His knee was throbbing again. "I expect our ships will be offshore Rio by April 1 or 2."

"All right," Braga said. "If your ships are there, we will move forward on April 2." God willing, he thought, most of his colleagues will have signed on by then. But he could not wait forever. Jango was certain to be moving forward, too.

Werner stood up. "I think we've done some good work, Antonio," he said. "I'll get back to you soon."

"I'll be waiting," said the marshal.

No653/64 TOP SECRET 25-3-64, 1723 hours

For McCone from ARMA, bcc H. Schwartz
Ref 647/64

1. *Further to REFTEL, I met this afternoon with Marshal Antonio Alberto Braga Neto, chief of Brazilian Armed Forces (roughly equivalent of the chairman of our Joint Chiefs of Staff). Braga is highly respected within the military and is the only Brazilian officer who we have told of the existence of Brother Sam. While he has some mixed feelings, he agrees that Brother Sam could be extremely helpful should the military need air cover or additional troops (although he believes that the coup will actually be carried out by telephone communications among the generals).*

2. *Marshal Braga did, however, impose four conditions for our participation:*

   a. We agree that the revolution is their fight, not ours, and that we not take any action unless expressly invited in.

b. *That the existence of Brother Sam remain secret unless Braga himself authorizes us to reveal its existence.*

c. *A commitment by us of no less than half a billion US dollars in Alliance for Progress financing annually.*

d. *That Jango not be assassinated.*

I explained to the marshal that I had no authority to make any of these commitments, that only the president had the authority to do so, and that for item c, congressional authorization would also be required.

3. *We also discussed the date the coup will take place. Braga stated that he did not yet have all the important officers lined up in support of the coup, but that the revolution would go forward on April 2, provided Brother Sam was offshore Rio by then.*

4. *It is my personal view that Braga's conditions a) and b) are acceptable. Condition c) is, of course, not doable without a congressional appropriation of funds. I believe Braga can be made to understand this, and that he will settle for a commitment by the executive branch to include the requested funds in its annual budget request to Congress.*

5. *The most difficult condition is d). I do not believe Braga will back down on this one, and see no advantage in trying to persuade him otherwise. As you know, Plan B has been approved by the president. Regrettably, Plan B is still the wisest course given the present situation in Brazil and the risks facing this country and the entire hemisphere in the future.*

6. *I would therefore propose that we proceed with Plan B notwithstanding the marshal's position on point 2d above. It should be possible to carry out Plan B without revealing who is doing so. We have the necessary skills available here in house to permit*

us to proceed. Carrying out the mission from this location will provide us with additional flexibility and knowledge and assure that the task will be carried out before or during the coup in a manner that cannot be traced to us. Use of our personnel here, under my supervision, should assure that the job is done right (unlike the recent botched effort in Cambodia).

Meanwhile, Brother Sam should continue its present course at full speed ahead to assure arrival no later than April 2.

—Werner

CHAPTER 28

General Werner arrived at the ambassador's office at precisely 5:00 p.m. Carter let him cool his heels in the waiting room for half an hour before he told Joannie to show him in.

"Sit down, Otto" he said. "I trust you have the information I requested?"

Werner sat down heavily in Carter's leather easy chair. "Well," he said, "I'm afraid we can't calculate Brother Sam's ETA without knowing exactly where Brother Sam is at the moment, and we don't know that."

"And why the hell not?"

"I've asked for it, sir, but we've had no response from the navy. The Pentagon says they don't have that information, sir. They say I need to get it from Admiral Whitcroft on the carrier. And the admiral insists I have to get it from Washington."

Carter knew Admiral Whitcroft. He was enough of a horse's ass that he'd probably say just that.

"All right, what's the *Forrestal*'s hull speed?"

"Thirty-three knots, sir."

"All right, Otto," he said. "How many aircraft does the *Forrestal* have on board?"

"Her capacity is ninety aircraft, planes, and choppers."

Carter stood up and walked to the window. "I'm not asking for her capacity, General," he said quietly. "You know damn well what I'm asking: How many planes does she actually have on board? I believe I made that clear to you this morning." The quiet of his voice belied the rage that was underneath. Werner did not miss it.

"I'm afraid I don't know, sir," Werner said. "Each service has its own security system and those aircraft belong to the air force. The air force will not provide that information to anyone who doesn't have a clearance under the air force security system, and I don't have that clearance. My clearance is army."

"And nobody can override that rule?"

"The Secretary of Defense can, but he is playing golf with the president in Texas. It was impossible to reach him."

Carter sighed. "And what about the troops? They're army, right? Like you, General."

"I'm afraid not, sir, they're marines. The Marine Corps has the same type of rules. And I'm not cleared under their system either."

"That's idiotic," Carter said. "But there are *some* aircraft, and there are *some* troops aboard, and they are United States Marines, right? Or am I to understand that the troops that aren't there aren't marines?"

Werner was silent.

"That's a question, General," Carter said. Carter thought he could see Otto's knee throbbing again under his pants. And then, without meaning to, he exploded.

"Goddamn it, Otto, you are going to answer that question or I will call the president, wherever the hell he is, and have your ass court-martialed for refusing to answer questions relevant to the national security of the United States, which are being put to you by a representative of the commander in chief. Are you going to answer or aren't you?"

There was a long silence. "All right," Werner finally said. "There are choppers on board the carrier, and perhaps some F-14 fighters. I don't know how many planes there are altogether, maybe eight or ten. Perhaps Washington will tell you—they won't tell me. There are perhaps half a dozen choppers."

"Troops?" said Carter.

Werner nodded his head. "Yes," he said. "The *Forrestal* can carry up to 3,826 enlisted men and 550 officers. I don't know how many of them are actually on board, maybe a few hundred."

"Where did you get your information?"

"I can't tell you that," Werner said. "I swore I wouldn't reveal my source. He did me a personal favor so I could get the information to you."

There was a long pause. "All right," Carter finally said. "Get the hell out of here before I change my mind."

It took him some time, and a glass of scotch from his lower desk drawer, to calm down. Part of what Otto had said made sense. If he didn't know where the flotilla was located, he couldn't project the ETA of its arrival at Rio. That much was true. But he simply couldn't believe Otto didn't know where the flotilla was located or that he couldn't find out.

And there were, in fact, troops and aircraft aboard. It didn't really matter just how many. In any case, it was plain that the United States intended to support the generals not only with petroleum, but with aircraft and marines. He assumed that if they weren't needed, both would be kept below decks and no one would be the wiser. That explained why they had sent the *Forrestal*, the largest aircraft carrier in the entire US fleet. You wouldn't send a "few hundred" troops, a mess of choppers, and warplanes on a smaller ship without risking being spotted. That would be no problem on the *Forrestal*. But the *Forrestal* will never reach Rio, he thought, it will either turn around before it enters Brazilian waters or it will be at the bottom of the sea playing with Yemanja.

What he really needed to know wasn't the number of troops or aircraft on board the *Forrestal*. He needed to know where she was and what her course was. He knew her hull speed, so with that data, he could calculate when she might enter Brazilian waters. Maybe not exactly, but close.

"Joannie," he said, "I want you to find me an admiral called Whitcroft or Witless or Halfwit or something. He's floating around the Atlantic somewhere on an aircraft carrier called the *Forrestal.* Get him for me if you can, please."

Joannie had Admiral Whitcroft on the radio fifteen minutes later.

"Admiral," Carter said, "this is Anthony Carter, United States ambassador to Brazil."

"I know who you are," the admiral said.

"That's good, I know who you are, too." Carter thought to himself: and you're clearly an asshole. But he was also the only possible source of the information he needed. "Admiral," he said, "I need your help. Can you tell me your current position?"

"I can," Whitcroft said, "but I won't. That information is classified."

"I am cleared for Top Secret," Carter said.

"Not by the navy."

"What do you mean, 'Not by the navy'?"

"You are State Department. We have our own security system. I can reveal classified information to someone outside our system only with authorization by the Pentagon."

"How long will it take you to get authorization?"

"About a week," Whitcroft said. "Maybe ten days."

"Look, Admiral," Carter almost shouted. "This is essential to the national security of the United States, if not the world. The outbreak of nuclear war between the United States and the Soviet Union may depend on your present location. That's all the information I need, but I need it now, not when your bureaucrats decide I can see it, sometime after half the world has been blown to hell."

There was a pause. "Mr. Ambassador," the admiral said, "I am terribly sorry, but I am afraid I cannot help you. I have just reread the applicable navy regulation. Part IV, Chapter 16, Section 16.43(b) reads—"

"I don't give a shit what it reads," Carter shouted into the phone. "And you can shove your regulations up your pompous ass!"

He hung up. Well, he thought, at least Otto wasn't lying. And telling the admiral to shove it had been more fun than anything else he'd done all week.

Goulart was scheduled to make a major speech at the Automobile Club in Lapa later that evening. Maybe the best idea, Carter thought, would be for him to attend and distract himself from thinking about Brother Sam for a while. Besides, the speech was important, it could well determine whether the president would survive, both politically and physically. A moderate talk that distanced him from his Communist sympathizers might rescue him from assassination. A radical leftist speech would have the opposite result. He decided to go, although he was concerned that he might be recognized as the American ambassador. In the back of his closet he found the false mustache that hadn't fooled Marina and glued it on. Then he drove the Fusca to the Automobile Club.

He needn't have worried about the mustache. By the time he arrived in Lapa around eight, there were more than three hundred army corporals and sergeants milling around the hall, drinking *chopp*, slapping one another on the back, and not listening at all to the speakers who were filling up the time from the podium as everyone waited for the president to appear. Carter found a seat in the last row.

Jango swept into the hall with his entourage at 10:30. The crowd roared its approval as he moved down the aisle surrounded by a coterie of cabinet secretaries, generals, corporals, sergeants, politicians, and hangers on, stopping every few feet to greet his friends and admirers as he went. Red flags bearing the hammer and sickle appeared in the hands of his supporters—civilian and military—all around the hall. The non-commissioned officers were particularly noisy, shouting *"Manda brasa, presidente"*—Give 'em hell, President! On the whole, Carter thought, it was one helluva welcome.

It took Jango almost half an hour to make it through the crowd and up to the podium. He waited for the crowd to quiet.

"I am here to serve our people," Jango said, *"And we will not be defeated."* Pandemonium. A few of the non-coms leaped up on their chairs wildly waving their red flags. Around them, everyone rose to their feet, cheering. "We will not be defeated," Jango shouted again above the noise. The crowd went wild.

"The current crisis in this country," he continued when the crowd calmed down, "was created by a privileged minority with their eyes on the past, afraid to look to the future. We will open up our democracy to millions of our fellow citizens."

More cheers.

The heat was growing oppressive as Jango went on. Carter thought about taking a brief walk out into the night, but that was unlikely to be much better. He began to doze.

"If you, the officer corps of Brazil, ask me where all these resources come from to support the powerful campaign against me, for the extraordinary mobilization against me, I tell you that this money comes from the illicit remittance of money of the foreigners who exploit our people, money tainted by the interests of the international oil cartel, and by foreign powers who seek the overthrow of our government by means totally repugnant to our constitution." Suddenly Carter was wide awake. "I warn those countries and their representatives to keep their hands out of Brazil." My God, Carter realized, that was aimed at him, and at Washington. Jango was practically inviting invasion by the United States.

"I will not permit a coup by Brazilian reactionaries nor by foreign powers," the president continued. "The coup we seek is one of basic reform, so necessary for our country. We do not want the Congress closed. On the contrary, we want it open. Open and sensitive to the fair demands of our people.

"The people of this country must know, having heard and seen us here on television, that there shall be no coup against this government. We shall not permit a coup against the wishes of our people."

Jango's speech was over. The hall burst into thunderous applause. Red flags waved in the air. "Give 'em hell, President!" someone shouted again, then a few began to chant and before long, the entire hall became a frenzy of soldiers chanting "Give 'em hell, President." Carter felt a little nervous, but no one was paying him the least attention. All eyes, all the energy was focused on Goulart. The demonstration took almost half an hour to fade away. Carter was heading toward the door when he saw Otto talking with one of the non-com officers. Carter made his way over to his military attaché.

"Otto," he said, "what a surprise to see you here."

"It's a surprise to see you here, too, Mr. Ambassador," Werner replied with a smile. "A most pleasant surprise."

"Let's talk a little about what's happening," Carter said. "I'd like your views."

"You mean tomorrow?" Werner said.

"No, now. I don't think this can wait until tomorrow. I think we'd better confer tonight."

"Here?"

"No, at the embassy. I have my car."

"I'm not sure it's wise for me to be seen leaving in the US ambassador's car. My contacts, you know."

"I came in the Fusca," Carter said. "It's just around the corner."

They rode in silence the few blocks to the embassy. The marine guard, at attention behind his desk at the door, let them in. They rode up to Carter's office in silence. Carter flicked on the lights.

"Whiskey, Otto?" Carter asked.

Werner looked relieved. "Love one," he said. "Neat."

Carter sat down behind his enormous desk. "Sit down, Otto," he said. "So, what did you think?"

"A powerful speech," Werner said. "His amnesty for the sailors after their demonstration on March 16 cemented his support with the navy. I think he's now assured of support by the army non-coms as well. That combination is pretty hard to beat."

"But it was a pretty radical speech, don't you think?"

"Well," Werner said, "maybe so, but it was a powerful speech."

"Won't it just make matters worse for him with the generals, and with Washington as well?"

"There are some generals against him—like Braga and Medici— and some who are still with him, Cordel, for example. I have no knowledge about them," Werner said.

"All right, Otto," Carter said. "Enough chitchat. I'm asking you again. What's the date that Brother Sam will arrive in Rio, if it arrives?"

"What do you mean, if it arrives?"

"What date, Otto?"

"I've already told you sir, I don't know."

"Bullshit!" Carter said. "If there's anybody in this benighted country who knows that date, it's you. I am the ambassador of the United States of America, Otto, and I need to know that date."

Carter turned in his chair, took down the picture of the president, spun the combination, and opened his safe. He took out his draft cable to Washington and passed it across the desk. "It hasn't gone out . . . yet, Otto. I'd rather not send it."

Werner slowly read through the cable, then set it down on Carter's desk. "You son of a bitch," he said quietly. For a moment, Carter thought his military attaché might punch him.

"Yes," Carter said. "But I don't see any other way to get the information I need."

"That's blackmail," Werner said.

"I know," Carter said. "Now when is that flotilla going to arrive offshore Rio? Believe me, I don't want to destroy your career. But this is more important than you or me. I get an answer to my questions right now, or that cable goes out. It's in the cable room already, waiting to go. All it takes is an instruction from me."

"I don't know. It depends on the current, tides, wind," Werner said quietly. "You'll have to talk with Admiral Whitcroft. Good luck with him. He won't tell me a thing."

"All right, Otto," Carter said. "Just one more question. When are your guys going to kill Jango? Don't tell me you're not CIA, Otto. I don't give a damn what you tell me about that. Whatever you say is probably a lie. But I'd like to hear what you have to say."

"How would I know that if I'm not CIA?" Werner said. "And I'm not."

"All right, as the lawyers say: Let me rephrase the question. What's the date that Jango will be killed, regardless of who does it?" Carter picked up his draft cable and slid it back and forth between his fingers. "You know, Otto," Carter said, "maybe I know you better than you realize. And I don't think you like assassinations any better than I do. You're just not willing to buck Washington if your career may be at stake. You're not alone in that. A lot of people feel that way. I'm giving you a chance to do what you feel is right. As far as Washington knows, I could have gotten the information anywhere. I can tell Washington I got it somewhere else, or I can tell them I got it from you."

Werner stared at him. "I don't know," he said, "And I don't want to." He stood up and limped to the door.

"Thank you, General," Carter said softly. He picked up the cable. "For both our sakes, Otto," he said, "I hope you told me the truth."

So much depended on when the flotilla might arrive in Rio. Nuclear war could break out that day unless the flotilla never arrived in Brazilian waters, or the coup had happened first. So much depended on where Brother Sam was now, but Carter didn't know that, and as long as Whitcroft remained as stubborn as a mule, there was no way for him to find out.

Or was there? It was crazy, but just maybe. . . . Carter looked at his watch. A little late to call. Still, the flotilla was moving. He couldn't afford to wait until morning. He flipped through his Rolodex, found the card he wanted, and dialed the number.

"Yes," a heavy voice answered.

"Ivan," Carter said. "I'm sorry. I know you're asleep, but I need your help."

The phone sputtered some noises which sounded like Russian profanity. "I'm sorry, Ivan," Carter said again. "I wouldn't wake you if it weren't important."

"What time is it?" the Russian demanded.

"Two o'clock."

"a.m.?"

"Yes."

"What in hell do you want at 2:00 a.m.?"

"I need to know where our flotilla is located."

"What?"

"I need to know where our flotilla is located."

"Are you crazy? You wake me up at 2:00 a.m. to ask me where your own flotilla is located? You must be insane."

"Well, it does sound crazy, Ivan. But I can't find out anywhere else, so I've had to come to you. It's important."

"At two in the morning. You are crazy."

There was a click and the line went dead.

General Werner sat at his cable machine. "No.654/TOP SECRET 30-3-64 0126 HOURS" the machine wrote for him. The rest he wrote himself.

For McCone from Werner
Ref 653/64

Further to REFTEL, AMB continues to vigorously pursue informa-
tion regarding location of Brother Sam, as well as planned date
Plan B, even resorting to attempted blackmail directed at myself. It
is becoming increasingly urgent that AMB be removed from scene
ASAP, until revolution has successfully taken place and Plan B

has been carried out. Our prior recommendation that he be called to Washington for consultations appears to have been unsuccessful. Our contact at Pan Am reports that his reservation is for April 3. That is clearly too late.

I believe the time may have come to implement Plan K so that AMB will be out of the way until revolution is over, at which time he will be released unharmed. We will, of course, proceed with absolute secrecy and take all possible steps to assure that AMB not be harmed in any way. I personally will do everything necessary to assure that USG cannot be connected with the project in press or elsewhere and will be available to take over other embassy functions to the extent required.

I await your instructions.

Regards,

ARMA

Washington's response arrived at 1000 hours. "Bald Eagle has approved your proposal," it read. "You may proceed Plan K. Regards, McCone."

CHAPTER 29

It had been bad enough, Carter realized, to wake up the Russian ambassador at 2:00 a.m. It would be just as bad to wake up Marina at three. Besides, he was exhausted. He would never be able to make love. So he had decided to sleep at the residence. He arrived at the embassy a little after eight thirty in the morning.

Joannie did not look happy. "They called from the palace at 7:30 this morning," she said. "The president's secretary said that you were 'summoned' to be at the palace at 9:00 a.m. That's the word they used: 'summoned.' It's 8:45 now."

"All right," he said to Joannie. "Please call Joaozinho and have him bring the Caddy around front, with the flags and all. And call the palace and tell them I'm sorry, but I'll be a few minutes late." I wonder what the hell Jango wants at this hour of the morning, he mused.

Traffic was better than usual, and he actually arrived at the Palace by 10:30. He needn't have bothered. Jango left him cooling his heels for over an hour. When he was finally shown into the president's office, it was almost noon.

Goulart had fire in his eyes. "Sit down, Mr. Ambassador," he ordered, "and explain to me exactly how your government is conspiring with our military to overthrow the government of Brazil."

Carter was at a loss for words. He knew of no conspiracy between his embassy and the Brazilian military. He did not know what Otto

Werner or Harry might be up to, but Jango would never believe that. Or was Jango referring to Brother Sam? "I'm sorry, Mr. President," he said. "I don't know of any conspiracy."

"Don't lie to me, Anthony. Your people are working with the very officers who are preparing a revolution against me. And if need be, if you continue with these activities, I will break off diplomatic relations with the United States and send you all packing. And I'll send you first, persona non grata!"

"I'm not sure I'd do that, Mr. President," Carter said. "I may be the only friend in the United States government you have left."

Goulart turned his back on Carter and stomped onto the balcony. Carter followed him.

"Can you tell me a little more of what you are talking about?" Carter said. "What conspiracy?"

"You must know this. Your army attaché met with Marshal Braga yesterday afternoon at the Ministry of War. He was there for almost an hour. My people could not overhear most of what was said—something about someone's brother."

"Yes?"

"There was also some conversation about an assassination."

Oh my God! Carter thought. Were they getting ready to do it? Should he have showed Jango that part of the secretary's cable when it came in? Would that have done any good?

"General Werner doesn't work for me," he said. "He's the army attaché."

"Or maybe he's CIA?" Goulart said.

"Maybe. They don't work for me either."

"But you know what they are up to?"

"Not always." There was a long pause. "You remember my last visit when I gave you a list of our demands: breaking relations with your labor supporters and firing your cabinet?"

Goulart nodded.

"And you told me to tell our president to shove his ultimatum up his ass? That wasn't wise, Jango. I did tell him. That probably wasn't wise either."

They both smiled.

"Washingington said you have to get the Communists out of your cabinet, at least for now. Our president would like to see you on our side, but there's no chance of that if the Communists are there."

Jango glared at the American ambassador. "On the same side, you and we? And the ultimatum you gave me last time you were here. Does that still stand?"

"Yes."

There was another pause.

"Yours is an evil government," the president finally said.

"Governments often are," Carter said. "Ours is probably no worse than most. I do what I can to point my government in the right direction, but I don't always succeed. They may or may not listen to me. Actually, I am little more than a messenger boy for Washington and a reporter of what's going on here, masquerading under the fancy title of 'ambassador.' That's what ambassadors do. They are not presidents."

"So, your people intend to assassinate me and kill my family?"

"I don't know, Jango. It's possible. . . . "

"When?"

"I don't know that either. In the past, if there was a coup, the assassinations usually happened during the coup. Or the day before."

"Can you find out when?"

"I am trying. Both the CIA and our military know that I am personally against our taking part in any coup, whether by the military or by you, from the left. They are, of course, on the side of the generals. And they are being careful to keep me in the dark."

"It would be very helpful if I knew the date," the president said.

"I'm sure it would. It would be very helpful to both of us. I certainly will let you know if I find out."

The fury returned to Goulart's face. "My family. . . . " His voice trailed away.

Yes, Carter thought. It wasn't just evil, it was obscene.

"Jango," he said, "perhaps it would be wise to get them out of here now, before anything happens."

"Yes," Jango said. The fire had gone out of his eyes as quickly as it had entered them. His shoulders had collapsed.

"And try to keep a low profile yourself, just for a little while," Carter added.

"I am still the president of this country," Goulart said. "I will do whatever I need to do for my people. No matter what your CIA would like."

Jango had grounds to be angry, Carter thought as he rode back to the embassy. What the hell was Otto talking with Braga about? Brother Sam? He had better make a call on the marshal himself. He might even find out something useful.

Joannie was at her desk when he arrived. "See if you can get me an appointment with Marshal Braga," he said. "As soon as possible." Although Otto wouldn't tell him when the flotilla would arrive in Rio, maybe he had told the Brazilians. The trick would be to get Braga to tell him, even though the flotilla was Carter's own government's.

"Yes, boss," Joannie said. She was back five minutes later. "He'll see you at noon," she said, "at the War Ministry, sixth floor."

General Amaral and three other officers were in the elevator when it stopped at the ground floor. Carter had met him once at an Independence Day event, and had found him less than brilliant. But he was a full general in the Brazilian Army and a potential leader of the coup.

"General," he said warmly, "how nice to see you. And isn't the weather lovely?"

Amaral clearly had no idea who he was. "Yes," he said, "but it's supposed to rain."

"Did you see the Flamengo-Fluminense game last night? Wasn't Robertinho incredible?"

"My television's broken," the general said.

The elevator was mercifully coming to a stop at the sixth floor. "I'm so sorry," Carter said. "Well, it was very nice to see you, General. *Ate logo.*"

"Ate logo," the general said.

Braga kept him waiting for almost half an hour. He got up out of his chair when Carter entered his office. Carter had met him several times before and come to respect his intelligence and integrity, even if he was a military man. If any of them was going to take over after the coup, he preferred it be this one.

"Good afternoon, Mr. Ambassador," the marshal said. "Please sit down. What can I do for you?" He sat back down behind his desk and almost disappeared.

"I won't beat around the bush," Carter said. "My government would be interested to learn. . . . "

"Bush?" the marshal interrupted. "What bush?"

"Oh, I'm sorry," Carter said. "Figure of speech. We would be interested to learn how the plans of the democratic forces are progressing. What your timetable might be."

The marshal looked pleased. "Your president has already decided on my questions? That's good news indeed. At least I hope it's good news. What did he say?"

Carter was perplexed. What questions? He was not aware of any questions. But it wouldn't be wise to let Braga know that.

"I'm afraid we don't have the answers as yet. The president is on vacation in Texas and it takes some time for messages to get through to him. But Washington has raised some questions about how soon the democratic forces plan to move ahead once your questions are answered."

The marshal looked surprised. "I already told General Werner," he said. "We will move when your flotilla has arrived and our generals are ready to proceed. Surely he told you that?"

"Yes, of course," Carter said. "But when do you expect that to happen?"

"You mean when will our officers be ready?"

Carter held his breath. "Yes," he said, "and when do you expect Brother Sam to arrive in Rio?"

Braga stared at him. "You mean you don't know that?" he asked.

Carter looked back across the desk. "Of course I do," he said. He hoped he looked persuasive. "But my government wishes to know the date yours will be prepared to move ahead."

Braga looked perplexed. "How would I know?" he said. "I told General Werner and I'm telling you: I do not plan to move until your flotilla arrives in Rio, our generals are ready, and our conditions have been met. It is your flotilla, not ours. You must know exactly where it is and when it will arrive. At least General Werner does. Perhaps you should ask him. Now, if you will forgive me, Mr. Ambassador I have a great deal to do, as I am sure you can imagine."

"Yes, of course," Carter said. "You have been more than generous with your time."

His limousine was waiting in the patio. "Embassy," he said to Joaozinho.

CHAPTER 30

The embassy elevator seemed to take an eternity to reach the seventh floor. Joannie was waiting for him when he stepped out.

"Did Ambassador Sverdlov call?" he asked.

"No, chief."

"Call him. Tell his secretary I'll pick him up at the Teatro Municipal at noon.

"OK, boss," Joannie said. "But I don't think he'll go for it."

Carter was waiting in front of the theater in a 1948 green Buick taxi twenty minutes later. Sverdlov wasn't there.

"Drive around the block," he said to the driver. It took another twenty minutes in the noonday traffic to circumnavigate the block. The Russian was still not there. The driver smirked at him.

"I don't think she's coming," he said.

"Shut up," Carter said. "And go around again." Another twenty minutes. Ivan was still not there. Carter stepped out of the taxi just as the Russian appeared out of the mass of humanity that was crossing Avenida Rio Branco.

"Get back in the car," Sverdlov ordered. "Botanical Gardens," he said to the driver. Why the Botanical Gardens? Carter wondered, but he said nothing. They drove through Botafogo in silence. This country is so beautiful, Carter thought, why are the two powers we represent getting ready to turn it into a nuclear wasteland?

The car turned in from the Lagoa, the huge lagoon that spread between Corcovado and the beach, and stopped at the main gate of the tropical gardens. Sverdlov motioned for Carter to follow him through the gate and the main promenade, with the royal palms on either side. Three quarters of the way down, he turned right on a narrow gravel path and sat down on a wooden bench under what looked like some banana trees. He motioned for Carter to sit next to him.

"Isn't it beautiful here?" the Russian sighed. "So peaceful."

Carter nodded.

"I'm sorry about last night," Sverdlov said. "Usually it's the Kremlin that wakes me in the middle of the night."

"*I'm* sorry, Ivan. It's just. . . . "

The Russian waved the explanation away. "Oh, it's all right," he said. "But it would have been nice to get a few more hours of sleep before we blow the world to hell."

"I understand," Carter said. He looked at the palm trees towering overhead. They must be one hundred years old, he thought. And what would happen to them now? He turned to the Russian. "Your submarines must know where—"

The Russian cut him short. "29°, 74' west longitude," he said, "8°, 85' south latitude, when I left the embassy."

"What?" Carter gasped.

"8°, 85' south. Off Recife I would guess. That means your flotilla will arrive in Rio roughly 44 hours from now." He looked at his watch. "That's 10:00 a.m. on April 2, unless, of course, you find a way to turn it around before that."

Carter stared at the large Russian diplomat sitting next to him.

"So now you see why I couldn't answer your questions on the phone last night?" Sverdlov continued. "That information and the fact that we know it must have the highest classification of any secret in the history of the Soviet Union. That's why we are sitting here rather than in a taxi. I couldn't risk anyone hearing us, not even a taxi driver."

So that's it, Carter thought. Now he knew when doomsday was. But so what? He couldn't turn Brother Sam around. He wasn't even supposed to know about its existence.

The Russian seemed to read his mind. "You have to turn them around," he said. "Or do something else."

"Thank you, Ivan," Carter said as he stood up. "Thank you very much. But there's nothing I can do." That's it, he thought. Nuclear war. April 2, some time before 10:00 a.m.

"Sit down," Sverdlov ordered. He pulled two Cuban cigars out of his breast pocket. "Today is March 31. What if the coup were to happen tomorrow?"

Carter stared at him. "It is scheduled for April second," he said. "That's when Brother Sam arrives."

"I know, but what if the coup were to happen tomorrow, *before* Brother Sam arrives? The generals are *your* team. Just order your team to get going tomorrow, even if Brother Sam hasn't arrived yet."

"And then what?"

"Then your government orders Brother Sam to stop where it is until you find out the result of the coup. That just needs to be before it enters Brazilian waters."

Carter stared at his Russian counterpart. He was right, of course. The flotilla didn't have to arrive later than scheduled. It made no difference when Brother Sam arrived, so long as the coup happened first. Once the coup happened, there was no need for Brother Sam. It could simply turn around and go home. He just had to make sure the coup happened first. But how could he do that?

Why was Sverdlov being so helpful? Carter wondered. He was the Soviet ambassador. He worked for the Soviet Union, not the United States. Suddenly the answer was obvious. If Brother Sam hadn't arrived when the coup took place, there was a better chance that the coup would fail, and that Jango and his government would survive. That was very much in the Soviet Union's interest. That was Sverdlov's objective.

"Cigar?" the Russian said.

"You're sure it won't explode in my face?"

"Better than a nuclear torpedo."

The Russian held the two cigars out to Carter. "Here," he said, "You choose."

CHAPTER 31

Joaozinho was polishing the Cadillac when Carter arrived at the embassy. He needed to think about the problem where he would not be disturbed.

"I'm going to Siqueira Campos," he said. "I'll take the Fusca."

He took the Botafogo Beach route to Rua Sao Clemente, cut across past the cemetery on Real Grandeza through the Tunel Velho and turned into Siqueira Campos. Marina wouldn't be at the apartment, he knew. She would be out in Bangu at her factory until April 1. He would have the apartment to himself.

He spotted a car stopped some three hundred meters ahead of him the moment he emerged from the tunnel. Christ, he thought, an accident. Just what he needed. He slowed down to see whether he could get by. He couldn't. The car was stopped right across the middle of the road. There were parked cars on either side that blocked any possible passage. Several long-haired college kids stood on the sidewalk near the car. A swarthy older man stood nearby.

"Damn," Carter said out loud, "I'm going to be here forever." Maybe if he backed up to the tunnel and took Santa Clara instead, he would be okay. But he was too far down Siqueira Campos to back up all that distance, and he couldn't just turn around. The street was too narrow, and was one way. And there was another car—a vintage taxi—stopped behind him.

He had rolled almost all the way to the car in front of him when he recognized it. It was the same black 1949 Plymouth that had tried to overtake him at the tunnel a few days ago, the one Joaozinho had left behind at the curve. The right headlight was still smashed. He saw that several of the "students" had pistols in their belts. Two of them were nervously pulling them out. They were close enough that they couldn't miss him if they fired.

The road was blocked, but the sidewalk was mostly empty except for the kids. On the left side of the road, an electric pole blocked any possible passage. On the right the kids stood watching. Next to them, a cart full of bananas, pineapples, and lemons stood abandoned by its owner.

"Watch out, guys," Carter shouted out the open window. Then he put his hand on the horn and jammed the accelerator to the floor. The Fusca shot forward onto the sidewalk, hit the fruit cart, sending the fruit flying in all directions, skidded over into the gutter, and bounced back onto the street. In his rear window, Carter saw several of the kids running up the street. Two lay on the sidewalk screaming. It looked like one had a broken leg. Well, he thought, they're lucky they're still alive. There was fruit everywhere. The swarthy guy was picking his way through it to the Plymouth.

Carter laughed. It looks like a primitive painting at the Ipanema Hippie Fair, he thought. The swarthy guy had made it into the car and was starting up the engine. Christ, Carter realized, this isn't funny. He stepped on the gas pedal and the Fusca charged down Siqueira Campos. He could see the Plymouth racing down the street behind him. It was catching up. He ignored the red light at the corner, turned into Avenida Nossa Senhora de Copacabana on two wheels, cut off a large bus, and raced down the avenue at 110 kilometers an hour.

It wasn't enough. In his rearview mirror he saw the Plymouth had passed the bus and was immediately behind him. The driver was smiling. In his right hand was one of the pistols Carter had seen earlier. Rua Republica do Peru crossed the avenue about two hundred meters ahead, one-way against him. Carter slowed down and pointed his finger at the curb. The driver behind him nodded. Just before Rua Republica do Peru, Carter swerved hard to the right across the traffic on the avenue and sped into the one-way street, just missing a refrigerator truck coming the other way. The Plymouth jammed on the brakes and turned to follow him. Carter heard the sound of breaking glass as the bus crashed into the back of the Plymouth. He looked back in his rearview mirror. The bus had come to rest across the entrance to the street. The Plymouth lay on its side in the middle of the avenue.

At the beach, Carter turned left onto Avenida Atlantica. A block down stood the Copacabana Palace Hotel. Perfect, he thought. The place where he had his very first caipirinha in Brazil some years ago. The very place to have another one to celebrate his survival. The bar was empty except for one or two gringos, and a table in the corner with a small group of Brazilians talking business.

Carter ordered his caipirinha and sat back in his chair. What the hell was that all about? Who would want to kidnap the American ambassador? Surely not the military. The United States was its closest friend. Marshal Braga might prefer to deal with General Werner, but he would never stand for his people kidnapping the American ambassador, particularly when he was counting on Brother Sam's support. Kidnap the ambassador and Brother Sam might turn its guns on the generals, not Jango.

Jango's people weren't likely to try to kidnap him either. He was the best friend Jango had in the United States government and Jango knew it. Carter could be no help to him unless he was in the embassy working the levers of power in Washington. No, it hadn't been Goulart's people.

It couldn't be the Russians. Sverdlov wanted him to persuade the generals to move the coup ahead to tomorrow. Obviously, Carter couldn't do that if he had been kidnapped. No, it wasn't the Russians.

That left only his own people. He knew Otto wanted to get him out of the way. That was probably why they had called him to Washington for consultations. That had failed. Maybe this was the next step. The CIA had worked behind the back of American ambassadors before. In the Dominican Republic, for instance. And in Panama. But kidnap the ambassador? Even the CIA wouldn't do that!

Or would they? Who at the embassy was CIA? Harry, of course. But Harry wouldn't have the balls. There were a few people in USAID, a few at USIS, the press attaché, and the labor guys. Part of the political section, of course. But that was about it. Most of them didn't even speak Portuguese. None would have been trusted by Washington to kidnap the American ambassador.

Except Otto. Otto was certainly no fool. His Portuguese was near perfect. His relationships with the Brazilian military were superb; Braga listened more to Otto than to anyone else, even on the Brazilian side. The CIA had failed in several recent operations elsewhere. Its standing within the United States government was at an all-time low. That was probably why they had called Otto from Italy to Brazil to work with his old buddies in the Brazilian military who were planning the coup. Perhaps that was why they had invented Operation Brother Sam, even though the Brazilians didn't need it. In fact, the CIA probably needed it far more than the Brazilians did. And that was why they were trying so desperately to get him out of the picture. If the coup succeeded, he, the American ambassador, would be the hero, not the spooks. To restore their reputation within the US government, they needed to be the heroes, not Carter.

Otto personally needed him out of the way as well. Carter still had not sent his cable to Washington. Like any blackmail, his cable only worked so long as he *didn't* send it. But if he didn't send it because he *couldn't* send it, because he had been kidnapped, Otto was safe. Yes, Otto definitely had his personal reasons to want Carter out of his way, at least until the coup was over.

Carter ordered another caipirinha. Did it really matter, he
thought, who had tried to kidnap him? What mattered was what to
do next. The flotilla was going to reach Brazilian waters on April 2.
Marshal Braga was not willing to move until Brother Sam arrived and
his generals were all lined up. There was no way he was going to move
ahead until April 2. But by then, if Kruschev had his way, Brother Sam
would lie at the bottom of the sea.

One of the other generals had to move first. Amaral? Friseh?
Cordel? Might one of them be willing to move even if Braga wasn't?
Not likely.

The waiter brought Carter's caipirinha, then went to turn down
the TV. A political commentator was interviewing a reporter Carter
didn't know about the possibility of a coup. "Well," the reporter said,
"it could happen as early as tomorrow if—" The waiter turned the set
off. "Such crap," he said to Carter.

"Quick," Carter said, "turn it back on."

"Como?" the waiter said. Carter realized that in his haste he had
spoken to the waiter in English.

"Por favor," he said, *"Ligue de novo. Rapido."*

The waiter turned the set back on just as the commentator was
closing the show. "But of course we don't know what General Amaral
may do," he said. A commercial came on.

Carter stared at the screen. *"Pode desligar,"* he said to the waiter.
You can turn it off. He took a long swig of his caipirinha. *"Tem telefone?"*
he asked the waiter.

Joannie picked up the phone on the first ring. "Where are you,
boss?" she asked. "Everybody's been looking for you."

"I'm at the Copacabana Palace."

"Gosh, boss," Joannie said, "Don't you like the residence anymore?"

"I'm not here by choice. I want to spend the night here, but not
under my own name. They probably won't check me in without some
kind of document. See what you can beg, borrow, or steal—a passport
or something—but not from the spooks. Not from General Werner

either. Then get down here as soon as you can. We have some important work to do."

"OK, boss, I'll be down in two shakes of a lamb's tail."

She was at the hotel in less than half an hour.

"Did you get me some kind of a document?" Carter asked as soon as she sat down.

Joannie looked embarrassed. "It wasn't easy, sir. There weren't that many people around, and nobody likes to lend out their documents. But Stoney stumbled in looking for you just as I was about to give up hope, and—well, you know Stoney. He's such a sweet guy. He lent you his Brazilian ID card."

"You mean Stoney Wyndham, the sewage guy?" Joannie nodded. "His ID card? It has his picture on it." Joannie nodded again. "He's bald. He doesn't look anything like me."

"I know, boss, but I couldn't. . . . "

"It's OK," Carter grumbled. "We'll just do the best we can."

"Do you really need to check in, boss? Couldn't we just work here in the bar?"

Carter pointed toward the businessmen still talking in the corner. "We need things a bit more confidential than this," he said. "And I'd rather not drive back to the embassy right now. It's not that healthy out on the street."

Joannie looked puzzled.

"We'll work upstairs," Carter said. "Come on, let's see if we can get into this dump."

The desk clerk smiled as Carter arrived at his desk. "I'd like a room for the night," he said. "Facing the beach if you have it. Double."

"Of course, sir," the clerk said. He ran his finger down his list of empty rooms. "I have a nice room on the fifth floor, sir. It's on the front, with a double bed. Private bath, of course."

"That's fine," Carter said. "I'll take it."

The clerk smiled. "May I have your document, please?" he said.

Carter took out Stoney's ID and slid it across the reception desk, face down. The clerk turned it over. "It doesn't look very much like you, sir. Are you sure this is your document?"

Carter jerked his head toward Joannie standing a few feet away. "It's *not* me," he whispered. "We're married, but not to each other." He slid a 1,000 cruzeiro note across the desk. "You know how it is," he said.

The desk clerk expertly slipped the bill from the desk into his pocket. "That's fine, Mr. Wyndham," he said. "Your documents are in order." He leered across the desk. "Do you have any luggage you'd like to have taken to your room?"

"That's all right. We can get it."

"Very well. It's room number 514." He handed Carter the key. "Elevators are on your left. I wish you a pleasant stay. . . . "

The room was small, but with a magnificent view down across the beach to Posto 6. He could make out the Bar Atlantico at the end of the beach.

"Well," Joannie said, "What's up?"

"Okay," said Carter. "First, I need you to find the pilot, you know, the Air Force guy who flies me in the embassy plane from time to time."

"Yes, sir," Joannie said. "That'll be Colonel Schiffel. He lives over in Ipanema, on Rua Joanna Angelica, near the beach."

I wonder how she knows that, Carter thought.

"He needs to get the plane ready to fly me to Juiz de Fora, tomorrow morning early. But," he continued, "the plane has to be disguised somehow. Don't ask me how: Schiffel will need to figure that out. I don't want anyone to know that it belongs to the US Air Force. We'll fly out of Santos Dumont. And Joannie, no one needs to know where I'm going, or even *that I'm going.*"

"Yes, sir," Joannie said.

"That includes Villepringle and Gilbert." Gilbert was the US consul in Belo Horizonte. "And the spooks. And General Werner."

"Of course," Joannie said.

"I need an appointment as early after my plane arrives as you can get it with General Amaral. He's the commander of the Fourth Military Battalion in Minas Gerais. He may be a little hard to find, but I'll bet he's set up some kind of field headquarters outside Juiz de Fora. If you have any problem getting through to him, tell his adjutant that I need to talk with Amaral about the presidency of Brazil."

"Yes, sir."

"And if you can do it, get me a set of violin strings."

"A what?"

"You heard me. I'm also going to need an appointment with President Goulart this afternoon. Tell him it's about the cable that I showed him. And tell his secretary to go fuck himself."

"Okay, boss, anything else?"

"Nothing else. Just make sure nobody knows about my little trip."

Joannie looked sadly at the bed. "Are you sure, boss? There's nothing else?"

Carter looked out the window at the Bar Atlantico, way down the beach. "No," he said. "Nothing else."

CHAPTER 32

Carter was up and waiting when Joannie arrived the next morning. "Good morning, Mr. Wyndham," Joannie said. "I had to come in early. The ambassador had some work I needed to do."

"Wise guy."

"I found Colonel Schiffel, although he wasn't too happy to be woken up at five in the morning. He'll be ready as soon as he gets his flight plan approved and the fog lifts. It's pretty bad just now." Santos Dumont was almost always without ceiling early in the morning. "He's painted over the stars on the wings."

"All right," Carter said. "Tell him to stand by. What about Amaral?"

"He's in a tent somewhere south of Juiz de Fora. He's sending a car to pick you up when you arrive."

General Alberto Amaral Filho set down his violin with regret. He had been practicing the second movement of Beethoven's violin concerto when one of his sergeants came into his tent. He had played that movement seven times now, the sergeant said, and the troops were getting restless. Could he perhaps play some other movement for a little while? Cretins, the general thought, but he set the violin down.

What did the American ambassador want? His secretary had mentioned something about the presidency. What was that all about? What did the American ambassador have to do with the presidency of Brazil?

In any event, the ambassador should be arriving soon. He went to his closet, took out his general's hat and put it on. The ribbons associated with his many medals were already pinned to his uniform. He took out his tobacco and filled his corncob pipe. Then he put on his sunglasses and walked over to the mirror. The hat made him look at least three inches taller than Braga, although they were almost the same height. "Good morning, General MacArthur," he said to the mirror with satisfaction. He picked up his violin and started to play Beethoven's violin concerto, his pipe clenched in his teeth.

The sergeant shook the door of the tent. "Ambassador Carter is here, sir."

"I'm so sorry to interrupt you, General," Carter said. "Beethoven, isn't it? The violin concerto? You play it beautifully." He handed the set of strings to the general. "I thought maybe you could use these. Strings may be a little hard to get in Juiz de Fora."

Amaral set his instrument down. "You are truly a diplomat, Mr. Ambassador. But I am sure you have more important things to do in these trying days than listen to Beethoven, no matter how well played. What brings you to Juiz do Fora? And what can I do for you?"

"A great deal," Carter said. The general looked at him with curiosity. "I won't beat around the bush," Carter continued. "As I am sure you know, my government is extremely interested in the preservation of democracy in Latin America, and particularly Brazil. We are concerned that the present government may be leading Brazil down a slippery slope toward communism and possibly even some form of alliance with the Soviet Union. You are doubtless aware of the situation. It is with great regret that we have concluded that some action must be taken—not by ourselves, of course—to assure the continuation of democratic rule in Brazil. That assurance will not be present so long as the Goulart regime remains in power." The general nodded.

"The problem is to locate a true leader, someone with the intelligence and fortitude needed to take the steps required to preserve freedom and democracy in Brazil."

"What about Braga?" Amaral asked.

"Marshal Braga is, of course, an extremely fine officer. He seems reluctant, however, to step out, front and center, to lead an effort to overthrow the regime. This needs to be done now, not later."

"Cordel?"

"Another very capable and honorable officer," Carter said. "But also a friend of the president, and formerly the chief of his military cabinet as well as his minister of war. I'm afraid we could not count on him."

"Machado then?"

Carter laughed. "Courage? Intelligence? My government is very serious, General. We are aware of your brilliant role in the Cohen Plan in 1937, and the assumption of power by Getulio Vargas. We are aware of your courage, your brilliance, and your commitment to democracy."

General Amaral let out a puff of smoke. He looked somewhat dazed. "What do you want of me?" he said.

Carter pressed forward. "What Brazil needs is someone who can lead its armed forces to overthrow Jango's regime before he can bring off a coup of his own. Our intelligence tells us that could happen as early as tomorrow. The person who could prevent that is you."

Amaral puffed nervously on his pipe. "How?" he said.

"By putting your tanks and your troops on the road to Rio. They're ready, aren't they? But you need to move quickly, before Jango does. And before Marshal Braga does." And, he thought, before Brother Sam does.

General Amaral reached down to scratch his balls. "Your secretary said something about the presidency?" he said.

"Oh, yes," Carter said, "the United States government will, of course, strongly back the leader of the revolution to be the new president of the Republic, assuming, of course, that the revolution is successful and democracy is restored to Brazil. You have my word on that."

Amaral's pipe had gone out. "I will carefully consider," he said. "My tanks will provide you with my answer by tomorrow. Your people will just have to watch where they are."

Carter took his leave. He could hear the general's violin begin to play as he stepped into the jeep. It sounded faintly like a melody from Beethoven's *Emperor Concerto,* although that piece was for piano, not the violin. He must like the name, Carter thought.

CHAPTER 33

"**W**elcome back, boss,**"** Joannie said, when Carter arrived back at the embassy after three o'clock. "I tried to get you an appointment with President Goulart, but I couldn't get through. The phone won't even ring."

Well, Carter thought, Roberto had told him that was coming. "I'll drive up there without an appointment. Tell Joaozinho to put the flags on the Caddy."

I guess I'm a bit of a shit, Carter thought as Joaozinho pulled the car out of the embassy garage. The United States wasn't about to back Amaral, but he had to think it would. There was no other way. Brother Sam could reach Brazilian waters tomorrow or the next day. The coup had to go off before that. Braga wouldn't move until Brother Sam arrived in Guanabara Bay. But Amaral would. In fact, Carter thought, he was raring to go. And once he did, Carter had a chance, at least a chance, of persuading his president to stop the flotilla's forward movement until he knew how well the Brazilian military was doing without Brother Sam.

Joaozinho pulled the Cadillac into the garage under the presidential palace. Several soldiers with submarine guns stood by the elevator. "Ambassador of the United States of America," he said as he strode past one of them. "I have an appointment with the president."

The soldier looked dubious. "Ciao," Carter said as he stepped into the elevator and the doors closed.

Jango's secretary was waiting at the elevator door upstairs. "Why didn't you call?" he demanded.

"Because you haven't paid your phone bill," Carter said. He knew the secretary didn't speak English.

"Yes, of course," the secretary said in Portuguese. "Please sit down. You'll have to wait."

The wait wasn't long. "Good afternoon, Mr. President," Carter said as Goulart strode into the ceremonial room. "Isn't the weather lovely for this time of year?"

"Oh, let's cut out the nonsense," Goulart said. "No weather, no football, no women. What is it you have in mind?"

"Things seem a little unsettled," Carter said. "If you'll forgive me, in fact it is the weather. I saw some pretty big storm clouds on my way over here. Perhaps we should go out on the terrace to see them."

Goulart got up. "I guess you're right," he said.

It was a lovely evening, Carter thought as he walked out onto the balcony. Balmy, a bit of a breeze off the ocean.

"Well," the president said, "what do you have to tell me? Is your country sending soldiers to support Amaral? Is your CIA going to murder me tomorrow at dawn?"

"Amaral?"

"Haven't you heard? The coup has almost started. His troops and his tanks are on the highway outside Juiz de Fora. They haven't moved yet, but it looks like they are ready to move at any time."

"Are any of the other generals with him?"

"Hard to tell. Our goddamn phones aren't working."

"Braga?"

"We believe he's on the fence. He'd like to see me gone, but for some reason, it seems he's not ready to move just yet."

"How about Cordel?"

"I don't know. But he has a great deal of integrity, and he believes in the Constitution. He will stick with me unless he believes I am acting against the Constitution. And that is something I will not do. . . . So, Mr. Ambassador, what do you have in mind?"

"I don't know exactly where or when, Jango, but there is a chance that our CIA will try to assassinate you, maybe today; if not, probably tomorrow. They like to do it in advance of a coup. It's probably too late for today, so I would guess it will be tomorrow."

Goulart nodded.

"Can you get your family out of here tonight?"

"They're already gone."

"Good. So, we only have to worry about you. I'm going to get you out of here, Jango." Carter paused. "I'll be here at eight o'clock tomorrow morning. Can you drive a Cadillac?"

"Sure," Goulart smiled for the first time since Carter arrived.

"Okay," Carter said. "And you need to find yourself a chauffeur's uniform. It doesn't have to fit that well, so long as you can get into it."

"Doesn't sound very presidential."

"Look," Carter said, "would you rather be a live chauffeur for a few minutes, or a president who is dead forever?"

Goulart said nothing.

"Obviously," Carter said, "no one can know that we're doing this. No one at all." He walked back toward the doors into the presidential office.

"Anthony," Goulart said. "May I know why you are doing this? You are the ambassador of the United States of America, your country considers me a danger to the hemisphere, it wants me out of the way. "

"Yes," Carter said. "That is what my government wants, at least part of it. But it's not what I want. There are some things I can't buy, Jango, like torture or genocide or murdering the president of another country, or of your own. . . . "

Marshal Braga was not happy. He had always believed that Amaral was a damn fool. But not this much of a fool. It was too early to move. Brother Sam was still north of Salvador. General Werner had told him that it would not reach Rio until April 2. He needed Brother Sam. The troops on board were United States Marines, among the toughest soldiers in the world. And the aircraft: modern fighter planes and helicopters, and well-trained pilots. There was nothing even remotely similar available in Brazil. The armed forces of Brazil did not have any helicopters at all. Its fighters were fifteen years old. Marines? Forget about it. Without even knowing it, Amaral was pissing all of that potential support away.

And then there was General Cordel. The military could not win a revolution against Jango without Sao Paulo. He had to have the Third Army with him, and that meant General Cordel. But as far as he knew, Amaral had not even phoned Cordel. That's what Amaral himself had told him on the phone not half an hour ago.

General Friseh had not been much help either. He had suggested that Braga put his troops on the Rio-Juiz de Fora road now and wait. Amaral would take over a day to arrive. By that time Braga would know better than now which way the wind was blowing in the officer corps, and whether Braga should fight Amaral or join him.

But a fight could result in a civil war, Braga thought. He would have to talk to Amaral again, much as he hated to do it. He switched on his intercom. "Get me General Amaral," he said to his adjutant. "You'll probably need to use radio. He's in the field." He switched off the intercom. "With the rest of the jackasses," he said.

General Amaral was on the phone a few moments later. Braga could hear what sounded like tanks in the background.

"Alberto," the marshal said, "where are you?"

"What?" Amaral shouted. "I can't hear you. The tanks are very noisy."

"I know, where are you?"

"We're in Juiz de Fora, Antonio. We're going to Rio." Braga could hear him better now. Apparently General Amaral had moved away from his tanks.

"It's too early, Alberto. We aren't ready to move yet."

"What do you mean, it's too early? That's what you always say. Everything is always too early."

"We haven't all pulled together yet. You know, as the gringos say, we must all hang together or we'll all hang separately."

"What does hanging have to do with it?" Amaral asked. "Have you gone crazy?"

The marshal decided to let that one pass. "It's a figure of speech," he said, "Look, we can't move without Sao Paulo. Have you spoken with Cordel?"

"No, I have not."

"Then how can you put your troops on the road?"

There were a few moments of silence. "Look, Antonio, Sao Paulo is Sao Paulo and Rio is Rio. Sao Paulo is five hundred kilometers away. We can't wait for everyone. . . . We are on the road to Rio, you understand? Rio de Janeiro."

"But it is too early," Braga said again. "We have to wait."

"Wait for what? For what?"

For Brother Sam, Braga thought. Two more days and the flotilla will be off Rio, and the fool insists on moving now. But he couldn't tell that to Amaral. The whole country would know about it within twenty-four hours. "Help is on the way, Alberto," he said instead.

"What help? What help?" Amaral asked again.

The marshal could not think of what to say.

"Antonio," Amaral shouted over the noise, "do you have any children?"

"What?"

"I said, do you have any children?"

The marshal was puzzled. "Yes," he said. "A son, Paulo."

"Well, that's a miracle," Amaral shouted. "Since you don't have any balls. Either it's a miracle or you should worry about what your wife has been up to."

The sound of the tanks ended as the line went dead.

General Werner was not happy either. John Gilbert, the United States consul in Belo Horizonte and chief of CIA operations in Minas Gerais, had called to tell him that General Amaral was mustering his troops at the top of the road to Rio.

Werner picked up the phone and dialed the embassy radio room. "Get me Admiral Whitcroft," he said to the radio operator. "Classify the record on the call Top Secret."

Admiral Whitcroft was on the radio a minute later. "What can I do for you, General?" he said.

"Where are you?" Werner asked. "Exactly."

"Just a moment," the Admiral said. There was a brief pause. "28° 16' west longitude, 9° south. . . . "

Thank God, Werner thought. Somebody had told the fool to talk to him. "Never mind," he said. " And when are you going to arrive in Guanabara Bay? That's Rio de Janeiro. In Brazil," he added.

"Just another second, please." There was another, somewhat longer pause. "1000 hours, Thursday, April 2," the admiral said. "unless the Humboldt current, or maybe it's some other current, helps us along."

"Can't you get here any earlier? It's very urgent."

"Look," the admiral said, "the *Forrestal*'s displacement is 59,560 tons, her hull speed is thirty-three knots. In case you didn't know, General, hull speed is the fastest speed an oceangoing vessel can go. You should know that, General, even if you are army."

Go fuck yourself, you pompous ass, Werner thought. But he said only "Thank you, Admiral." and rang off.

Marshal Braga sat looking out the window at the gathering dusk. From his desk he could see the statue of Christ on Corcovado, the spotlights turning it brighter as night began to fall. He sighed. He didn't want to put his own troops on the road to block Amaral from coming down. Brazilians shooting at Brazilians was not the Brazilian way. But what choice did he have? If he could hold Amaral off until Brother Sam arrived, he could then let him come down to Rio de Janeiro and join the party. In any case, he had better make sure when Brother Sam was due to arrive. He switched on the intercom.

"Ask General Werner to come down," he said. "As soon as possible."

Werner had just the same worries. "What have you heard, Antonio?" he said as he strode into Braga's office.

"Nothing new," the marshal said. "Amaral is a fool. He doesn't have the arms, or even any trained troops. His tanks are a joke, I reviewed them a few weeks ago. He needs troops, equipment, arms, planes. All our armies are like that. And that's why I agreed to Operation Brother Sam. Where is the flotilla now, Otto?"

"As far as I know, it's at about 30° west longitude, 9° south, just off Recife. It should be here on the second."

"I wish it could be here earlier," Braga said.

"So do I, Antonio, but what can I do? I can't send a plane to pick up a 60,000 ton aircraft carrier and carry it to Rio."

The marshal stared at Werner balefully. "Well, what *can* you do?" he asked.

"Not much," Werner said. "Maybe drop some arms in by air, if you can tell me just what you need and where. But I'm afraid I can't do much more than that. Not troops, not tanks, not planes. We'll have to wait for Brother Sam for all that."

"Look" Braga said, "If the revolution fails, I want you to send Brother Sam back home. No one must ever know that we lost because we didn't wait for it. Your government must say that we never knew it existed.

"In fact, the same is true if we win. It will only hurt the reputation of your country in Latin America if Operation Brother Sam ever becomes known. And my own reputation as well. I will be accused of being a tool of the United States."

"We can classify that information," Werner said, "and try to keep it secret. But I can't promise it will work. We have laws which sometimes force us to give out information we'd rather keep secret."

"I understand," the marshal said. "But if we lose, at least don't let the people of my country know how close we came. We'd look like fools for not waiting for Brother Sam."

TOP SECRET
Werner to SecState

We are informed by Admiral Whitcroft that the Brother Sam task force will only arrive Rio at approximately 1000 hours on Thursday. By that time the revolution may be over and decided. In that event Brother Sam will be useless if the revolution has failed, and actually counter-productive if the revolution is successful, since the appearance of potential American military presence only makes the Brazilian military appear to be weaker than they actually are and tools of the United States. Accordingly, whatever the outcome of the revolution, I recommend that:

1. The existence of the task force remain secret; If the revolution is successful, we believe it is likely that Marshal Braga will become president. In the event that the existence of Operation Brother Sam ever becomes known, it is important that we protect him and other members of the Brazilian armed services by stating that none of them had any knowledge of the operation. This is also true if the revolution fails.

2. If the revolution fails, it may be argued by some within the armed forces that the failure was because the military did not wait for the flotilla. If necessary, we should state that the flotilla only left the Caribbean today, and would only have arrived here twelve days from now, too late to do any good, and too late to wait for.

3. As noted above, Brother Sam will not be here until Thursday morning. The military may need some small arms now. I will let you know ASAP precisely what is needed, and where and how they should be delivered.

4. We do not yet know what will happen in the next days. Admiral Whitcroft should be directed to proceed to Rio de Janeiro ASAP. (We understand that although hull speed of the Forrestal is thirty-three knots, the flotilla has been proceeding at a somewhat slower pace.) General Amaral may start the revolution from Minas Gerais before Brother Sam arrives. I shall keep you informed of whether and when Brother Sam continues to be needed. If it is not, the flotilla should return ASAP to its home port before its existence becomes known.

—Werner

There were a few streaks of light in the east when Harry let himself into Thornton's apartment. It hadn't been easy to get there: He had been stopped twice along the way, once by the military police, once in front of the governor's mansion.

The routine with the military police was the same as always. They asked for your documents, you put a one-hundred cruzeiro note in with your driver's license, and off you went.

At the governor's mansion, it looked, at first, a little more complicated. Several tanks were lined up on the road, their gun turrets facing the presidential palace. There were soldiers outside their tanks, smoking and talking. The sergeant came over to the car. "The road is closed," he said.

"I'm going through the tunnel Santa Barbara," Harry said.

"That's closed, too."

Harry pulled two hundred cruzeiros from his pocket, down below the window, and held them there, out of sight. "Are you sure?" he said.

"Very sure."

Harry added another three hundred cruzeiros to the bills he held in his fist.

The sergeant reached in the window. "All right," he said in a loud voice, "but only because your mother is sick. Don't come back this way. The tunnel is completely closed."

Harry drove through the tunnel back over the hill, down Rua Erfurt and into Parque Guinle from the back. A single tank stood at the top of the hill. There was no one there. Harry drove down the hill without stopping and into the parking lot. Thank God no one had been at the tank. He was ten minutes later than he wanted to be already. The foreigners who lived in Parque Guinle would not be up this early, but their maids might be arriving at any moment. It would be a pity to have to kill a maid. But he was lucky. No maid. He crept his way through the back door of the building, up the stairs, and into Thornton's apartment.

Nothing had changed. The magazines were exactly as he had left them on the floor, open to the same pages. No one had been there. There was no one in the park. He opened the front window and looked down. Thornton's body still lay crumpled behind the bushes. There was a faint, sickly sweet smell of rotting flesh. It was lucky, Harry thought, that Washington had given Code Green. Another day and Thornton might have begun to really stink.

Harry pulled down the blinds on the front window, pulled the khaki bag off his shoulder, took out the tripod, and carefully put it together. He tightened, then retightened the joints, and set the tripod down in front of the window. He slipped the cradle into the top of the tripod and turned it. He liked using a cradle. If you rested the front of the gun in the cradle, you could reduce the effect of body vibration by as much as fifty percent.

Then he took out the gun.

Harry looked at his Uzi gleaming in the morning light. It was beautiful. It looked to him like a giant metal penis, waiting for him to make it come. He stroked the barrel. "My sweet hard one," he whispered. He put the end of the gun in his mouth and ran his tongue around the barrel. Then he lay back down on the floor.

Harry opened his bag again, took out a round of ammunition, and loaded the gun. Then he set the rifle into the cradle. He looked outside the window. There was still no one in the park. Carefully, he opened the shade to just above the barrel of the gun, then opened the window to the same height. He lay down on his stomach and looked carefully through the scope. It was perfect. Across the park, he could see, clear as day, the nose on the statue of Roberto Guinle on the terrace of the Palace. Pity I can't see inside, he thought. But who needed it? He could see the cobblestones along the road. He could see the bolts on the tanks at the top of the road. He would be able to see Jango whenever he tried to leave the palace. No problem.

Harry lay down behind the gun. Now all he had to do was wait.

Joaozinho picked Carter up in the Cadillac at the residence at eight o'clock. Although he had only gotten to bed at one in the morning, Carter wasn't sleepy. After all, it wasn't every day that you went to save a president. Well, they may have ordered him to stay away from Brother Sam. But they hadn't said a word about saving Jango.

Maybe that wasn't in their plans at all. Maybe all they cared about was the coup. But he doubted it. Look at what the CIA had tried elsewhere in Latin America and in Asia as well. They hadn't been that successful, but they might well try again in Brazil. Practice makes perfect, he thought.

Joaozinho was speeding down Voluntarios da Patria heading toward the bay. He turned left onto the Botafogo Beach road, and into Rua Pinheiro Amaral. Carter could see the tanks in front of the Guanabara

Palace, the home and offices of Carlos Lacerda, governor of the state of Guanabara and sworn enemy of Goulart. The traffic was stopped.

"Drive over to the left," Carter said, "and keep moving slowly. Our flags are on, aren't they?"

Joaozinho nodded.

"Just smile as you drive around the tanks, and point to the flags. If they threaten to shoot us, stop."

The sergeant glared at them as the Cadillac drove up next to the tanks. *"Pare ahi,"* he snarled, "Stop there."

"Sim," Carter said in Portuguese, with what he hoped was a thick American accent. "And a lovely day to you, too."

"Eu falei para voce parar!" I told you to stop! The Caddy was almost around the tank. The sergeant was standing immediately next to Carter and starting to unhook the submachine gun on his shoulder.

"Thank you," Carter said, "you have a nice party too. . . . All right, floor it!" he shouted at Joaozinho. The Cadillac shot forward toward the tunnel, then spun on two wheels into Rua das Larangeiras. Carter looked back; the tanks were no longer in sight.

"Hey, boss," Joaozinho said. "That was fun. Want to do it again?"

"Thanks," Carter said. "But no thanks. You can take me to Parque Guinle on four wheels, please."

The massive stone gate into the park was open.

"Drive in," Carter said. "Up to the palace."

"Another palace?"

"Yes. The one behind us belongs to the governor. This one belongs to the president."

"There's a tank up there."

"Don't worry," Carter said. "There's only one; we'll get past that one too."

Harry recognized the Cadillac the moment it passed through the gate. "What the fuck?" he said. Oscar was supposed to put a tank a few meters down the street, out of sight of the gate, to keep unwanted cars away and to stop Jango's car from leaving if he were somehow to get past Harry. But apparently he hadn't done so. "What the fuck?"

The Cadillac moved up the hill along the road beneath him, toward the tank at the top of hill. Harry looked through the scope of his rifle. There was no one at the tank. Carter's car drove slowly past it, along the top of the hill, and into the Palace garage.

What the hell is Carter doing here? Harry wondered. Was he going to have to shoot that striped-pants son of a bitch as well? He put the gun back in its cradle. The car was out of sight in the garage. He would just have to wait.

Goulart was standing in his reception room when Carter arrived.

"Mr. President," Carter said. "It's good to see you. Isn't the weather lovely? Perhaps we should go outside?" He motioned toward the terrace.

The president looked at him. "Fuck 'em," he said. "If anyone wants to hear what I have to say, let them listen."

Carter was astounded. "Look, Jango—"

The president cut him off. "Anthony," he said, "You've told me that your people may be trying to kill me. Maybe mine are too. By the time DOPs or the CIA hear this, I will be either dead or gone from here. I assure you I am not going to sit here waiting. So let them go fuck themselves, as you people say."

Carter remained silent.

"Well, how are things going out there?" Jango said.

"You don't know?"

"No. Not really. They've cut off my phones. What's this that Dantas Castro tells me about Amaral?"

"I don't know," Carter said. "I hear he's put his troops on the road somewhere below Juiz de Fora."

"Why in the world has he done that? Isn't Braga in charge?"

"My consulate in Belo tells me Amaral wants to be the one who kicks off the revolution and gets all the glory. He wants your job, Jango."

The president snorted. "That horse's ass? Even your government wouldn't want him to be president of Brazil."

He has a point, Carter thought.

"Jango" he said, "Why did you include that attack on the United States, and on me personally, in your speech last night? I'm the one who's trying to save your ass, for Christ's sake, even if it costs me my job."

Goulart gazed at him. "I know," he said quietly, "that's why I did it. Your government could hardly believe that you were trying to save my life after they heard my speech."

He's right, Carter thought. "Payment in advance for services to be rendered?"

Goulart nodded.

"All right," Carter said. "I guess it's time for me to deliver. But I need your help. You know how to drive my Cadillac?"

"I already told you I did."

"All right. Would you please put on your chauffeur's uniform. Don't forget the tie."

Goulart walked out of the room. He's a gutsy guy, Carter thought. The United States may not like his politics, but that's no reason to kill him. There's never good reason to kill a president.

The door opened and Jango strode back into the room. His uniform looked a trifle small, but he had squeezed into it.

"Where's your cap?"

Goulart swore under his breath, left the room, and returned a moment later with the cap. It was much too small.

"Scissors?" Carter asked.

Goulart went to his secretary's desk and took out a pair of scissors. "Here," he said. Carter snipped the back of the cap and pulled it down over Jango's head. It was all right from the front and side, but looked like hell from the back. "It'll have to do," he said. Then he took his actor's mustache and a small jar of gum out of his pocket.

"What the hell is that?" Goulart said.

"It's a mustache," Carter said. "Just like Joaozinho's."

"Why do I need a goddamn mustache?"

"Because I'm the director of this play, Mr. President. Now, hold still." He affixed the mustache to Goulart's upper lip. "Okay, Mr. Chauffeur, let's go."

Joaozinho was sitting in the driver's seat when they arrived in the garage.

"I'm afraid you'll have to get out," Carter said. "The president is driving."

Joaozinho got out of the car. "Where do I sit?" he asked.

"You don't." Carter said. He handed Joaozinho a fifty-cruzeiro note. "Wait half an hour, then take a cab back to the embassy." He turned to Goulart. "Get in and close the window. I'll ride shotgun in the back. I don't trust this place. Drive slowly down to the lower gate, turn left, and take off down the Rua das Laranjeiras and into the Tunel Santa Barbara. Don't stop for anyone."

"Where are we going?"

"Galeao. You have a plane there, don't you?"

"Yes."

"Well, that's why we're going there. Let's go."

Harry watched Carter's car pull out of the palace garage and drive toward the tank at the top of the road going down the back. He could see a couple of soldiers there now. They waved the car past and the Cadillac continued down the front road toward him. Shit, Harry thought, what if Carter smells the body? But he could see that the windows of the car were closed. It's OK, he thought. The car was passing right underneath him now, moving slowly toward the gate. He could see Carter sitting in the back seat. But something was wrong. It was Carter's car for sure, and it was Carter sitting in back. But there was something wrong with the back of Joaozinho's head. Something was wrong with his hat.

"Fuck," Harry breathed, "That isn't Joaozinho. It's Jango!" He dove for his gun, brought the scope to his eye, and fired. The Cadillac lurched, then continued on through the gate. For the first time in his career, Harry had missed.

It was past eleven o'clock. General Amaral had planned on getting his troops on the road by nine thirty, but it just hadn't happened. First the phone call from Braga, pretty much the same as last night.

"We're not ready, we have to wait." What the hell was the man waiting for? And then Paes Araujo. That had been a much more agreeable call.

"Amaral," the general had said, "You heard Jango's speech on the radio last night?"

"Of course," Amaral said, although in fact he hadn't.

"It seems to me he's threatening us with a coup of his own against the Constitution."

"I agree."

"I hate it," Paes Araujo said, "but I think we have to move first."

"I agree with you, José."

There was a long silence.

"José?"

"I'm still here," General Paes Araujo said. "We have to move first to preserve the Constitution."

"Yes, yes, of course. I agree completely."

"We are behind you." Amaral heard a click and the line went dead.

I wonder which army that is, Amaral thought. A breeze blew toward him from the direction of the officers' mess bearing the smell of slightly putrid *picadinho*. At home he knew that Dorothea, his *mineiro* cook, was preparing *feijao tropeiro* with pork chops, one of his favorite meals. What the hell, he thought. An army fights on its stomach, particularly its generals.

"I'm going home for lunch," he said to his adjutant as he climbed into his jeep. "I'll be back by one."

Lunch wasn't quite ready when Amaral arrived home. There was some good *mineiro cachaca* in the house, a gift from a nearby farmer. He made himself a caipirinha as he waited for lunch.

Things were going just fine, he thought. Clearly Braga was not going ahead. Good! Paes Araujo was behind him. And best of all, the United States was behind him, and would make him president of Brazil when the coup was over. He deserved a drink and a good lunch! Surely, there was time for another caipirinha.

The *feijao tropeira* was superb, the beans cooked just the way he liked them—not too dry. And the *papo de anjo* dessert was sweet and syrupy and totally delicious.

A meal like that surely deserved a little nap. What difference did it make if his army marched on Rio a few hours later than he had planned?

CHAPTER 34

The light was fading behind Dois Irmaos when Carter arrived back in Rio and stopped at the embassy. He called Gilbert in Belo Horizonte. No, his consul said. General Amaral's tanks hadn't moved. They were still in Juiz de Fora at the top of the highway to Rio. It looked as if he was was waiting for Braga to move first.

Well, Carter thought, he had done the best he could. As it turned out, that hadn't been much. If Amaral had moved on Rio today, things might have been different. But he hadn't. And now, Brother Sam was sure to arrive in Rio in time for the coup, except that the Soviets would sink it first. Nuclear war was inevitable. There was nothing more he could do.

Marina was wearing nothing but a tight pair of jeans when Carter arrived at Siqueira Campos. "Welcome home, sweetheart," she said as she threw her arms around him. She kissed him, her bare breasts pushed into his chest, but his penis didn't respond like it usually did.

"What's the matter, Tony?" she said. "You're not sorry that I'm going to win against the generals at midnight? That your other mistress will be gone?"

Carter sat down on the bed. "You've won, darling." He said. "The coup hasn't happened yet, but it will happen tomorrow, and I'm done with it."

"You don't seem happy," she pouted.

"I wish I could tell you about all the things I tried to do, but I failed. And now it's going to turn out terribly. It could be the end of the world."

Marina stared at him, then her face wrinkled into a grin. "My God, Tony," she said, "you mean if you'd succeeded you would have prevented the end of the world? My own lover could do that? You've got a wonderful, strong prick, Tony, but strong enough to rescue the whole world?" They were both laughing now. "Maybe you're really Ogun or one of the other gods, not just the American ambassador."

Carter reached over to pull down the zipper on her jeans. "No," Marina said, "not yet. You can still play with your generals, if you want to, up until midnight. That will be April 1, what you call April Fools' Day. After that, we'll make love like we've never made love before. But before that, let's go have dinner. I'll show you one of my favorite places. Do you have your Fusca?" she asked. Carter nodded. "Good," Marina said, "I'll drive. It's not far." She disappeared into the bedroom.

A few moments later she re-emerged, having added a soft green blouse and green tennis shoes to her attire, and a deep purple and gold shawl. As usual, no brassiere. She looked sensational, Carter thought.

They drove through Copacabana, the sky growing darker as the shadows lengthened. "I want to get there before dark," Marina said as she tore through a red light on the Rua Toneleiros.

"Where are we going?"

"You'll see," she said, "In a minute we'll be going through the Corte de Cantagalo, which takes you from Copacabana to the Lagoa. It means the Singing Rooster. They say there used to be a large rooster who lived on a farm there and screwed all the chickens for kilometers around. With each one he screwed, he'd sing a few loud obscene love songs. It was quite terrible. Finally, the local residents asked the municipality to cut his throat. The mayor, who was a little hard of hearing thought they said "cut a moat." Why anyone would want a moat connecting Copacabana and the Lagoa is beyond me, he thought, but since

elections were coming up, he did it anyway. He carved the Corte de
Cantagalo right through the mountains. Later on, they put in a road,
the one we're on. "Look," she said, "there's the Lagoa." She turned left
and they drove along the side of the lagoon toward Ipanema.

"What happened to the rooster?" Carter asked.

"There's two versions," Marina said. "One says that he moved to
Pernambuco and died years later, while still fucking the local chickens
there. The other is that they chopped him up and served him with
garlic to the patrons of the Bar Lagoa. They called it *frango a passarinho*.
Marina had stopped in front of a restaurant with a huge, shaded terrace in front. "And that," she said, "is where we are right now."

Although the sun was setting behind Dois Irmaos, there was still
daylight shining on the statue of Christ on Corcovado on the opposite
side of the Lagoa. "Fritzchen," Marina called to one of the ancient
waiters, "could we have a table in the front please?"

"Of course," Fritzchen said. "For you, Marina, there's always a
table, wherever you like it."

Marina smiled at Carter. "Do you want to start with caipirinhas?
They're good here. And this one is on me."

The drinks came soon. "Here's to us," Marina said as she looked
into his eyes and clicked her glass with his. "To our."

"Our?"

"Yes," she said. "You add whatever words you want. Like love, for
instance."

Carter looked around the restaurant. Although it was still early,
it was full of young couples. None of them knew that a nuclear war
was coming.

Marina was chattering happily about the trip she wanted to
make. "Next week," she was saying, "before it starts raining again."

"Sure," Carter said. "Why not?"

"You don't even know where we are going to go," Marina said.

"No," Carter replied. "I'm sorry. I was thinking about something else."

"It's all right," Marina said. "Like I told you, you have until midnight to think about whatever you want. After that, you think only about me. And we'll go to Buzios."

"Okay," Carter said. "But why Buzios? It's beautiful, but there aren't any hotels."

"I know," she said. "But Brigitte Bardot has a lovely big house there. I went there once with a movie star from France. Why can't we stay there?"

"I don't know her."

"You are the United States ambassador," she said. "You can get to know her." That seemed to be that, as far as Marina was concerned. "Fritzchen," she called out to the waiter, "bring us some *weisswurst*, potato salad and sauerkraut, and some German mustard, please." She smiled at Carter. "This used to be a German restaurant," she said. "It was called Bar Berlin. They changed the name before the war, but they never changed the waiters."

The food was delicious and plentiful. By the time they finished, the sun had disappeared behind the Dois Irmaos. Marina looked across the Lagoa at the Christ, still glinting in the evening sun. "Let's go up on Corcovado," she said. "You've never seen my little factory. Maybe I can show it to you from up there. Come on, I'll race you to the car."

Marina drove fast around the Lagoa, through the old section of Botafogo where Carter had never been before, past the Largo de Amaral Square, and up the Rua das Laranjeiras. At the corner of Rua Alice, she stopped. "This used to be my stomping ground," she said. She drove slowly up Rua Alice and stopped in front of a large Victorian house that was painted pink. "That's where I began my career," she said, "when I was sixteen. It's still the best establishment in town. It's clean; new sheets after every job. The music is nice—you know, samba, bossa nova. In my day, the mistress was completely honest. She took us newcomers under her wing and paid us what we were entitled to."

Carter looked over at her. He had completely forgotten that she had been a prostitute when he met her just a few weeks ago.

"Everyone knows it as the Pink House," Marina continued. "Now and then, some guy would call it a 'whorehouse.' We would kick him out. It's much too fine to call a 'whorehouse.'"

Carter didn't want to hear any more, but he couldn't help himself. "How did you get there?" he stammered. "You were only sixteen."

"Momma," Marina said. "She worked there. She was still very beautiful then. She wanted to keep an eye on me, so she got me in, even though I was young and inexperienced. But I was beautiful, even then."

"Your mom brought you to work in a whorehouse?" Carter asked in disbelief.

"I told you," Marina snapped. "It's the Pink House, not a 'whorehouse'."

"I'm sorry," Carter said. There was a long silence. "You wanted to be a prostitute?"

"Sure," Marina said. "Momma made her living that way. She liked it. It's like Mozart—his father was a great composer. So was Bach's. My mother was a great prostitute."

Carter stared at her, "You mean—"

Marina cut him off. "You gringos are all the same. You think we have to hate what we are doing, that we are all miserable, mistreated, abused. You have never been a sixteen-year-old Brazilian girl, Tony, and never will be. Sex was fun, some variety was great, and you even got paid to do it. Nobody thinks it's wrong for a girl in Rio de Janeiro to have sex with her boyfriend if she wants to. . . . It's fine for her to get presents. . . . But if she gets paid money, suddenly it's all wrong?"

"But don't you have to have sex with guys you hate? There must have been some terrible guys, dangerous ones."

"Sure, but Momma was there to look after me. And the house always had a big, black bouncer to protect us. Actually, the bad guys never got in the door."

"You didn't mind sleeping with different men every night?"

"We didn't. Most of the clients were repeaters. And we only took them on if we liked them. A lot of them were pretty nice guys. They

just had an awful sex life at home, or maybe none at all. If you didn't
like a guy, you didn't have to sleep with him. There were always plenty
of other girls who needed the money. And we made all our johns use
condoms. If they didn't like that, we'd give them a blow job instead."

"But what about love?"

Marina looked at him. "Sex is one thing, Tony," she said. "Love
is another. I never loved any of my clients . . . until you. Come on.
Let's drive up to Corcovado. You can ask the statue of Jesus whether
that's true."

They drove up to the top of Rua Alice in silence, then turned left
and continued uphill, though the Tijuca Forest. "Look," Marina said
as they passed a miniature temple by the side of the road. On it was an
open bottle of cachaça, a small ceramic figure of a woman in a long
dress, and a candle that was still burning. "Macumba. I showed you
some before. This is new, the candle is still lit, and no one has drunk
the cachaça. That means good luck. Come on. You can ask Christ
about that, too."

By the time they reached the top of the road, it was almost dark.
"Hurry," Marina shouted over her shoulder as she ran up the steps to
the base of the statute. "I want to show you the factory." It was too late.
She looked down at the carpet of lights that rolled out to the north
as far as the eye could see. "It's way out there in the dark," she said.
"You'll just have to come out to Bangu to see it."

Carter watched the carpet grow brighter as the lights flickered on.
"I will," he promised. "I will. Soon."

Carter had never been on Corcovado before. You could see the
giant statue of Christ from everywhere in Rio de Janeiro, but he had
always been too busy to go up. When there were "important" visitors
from the States, he had sent Villepringle or a junior foreign service officer to take them to Corcovado, Sugarloaf, and the Garota de Ipanema
bar, where Jobim and Vinicius wrote "The Girl from Ipanema."

Carter looked down at the south zone. He could see it all, from
Copacabana to Ipanema and Leblon and beyond them, the black of

the sea. To his right, the bright lights of the Jockey Club and the flickering lights of the favela at the foot of Dois Irmaos.

"Look," Marina said, "we couldn't see Bangu but you can see my building in Siqueira Campos. See where those three streets come out of the Tunel Velho on the Copacabana side? The middle one is my street."

"I know," Carter said. He could almost see the telephone pole at the exit of the tunnel, the one Joaozinho had missed but the car behind them hadn't.

"We've had some good sex there," Marina said.

"Let's go home and make love now," Carter said.

"But we haven't asked the statue yet whether we'll be lucky . . . or whether I ever loved anyone else but you. I told you we had to do that."

"What do you mean, 'ask the statue'?"

Marina laughed. "The answers are really inside you, Tony," she said, "not in the statue. He's a big piece of stone. But go ahead and ask him. He'll answer the truth."

"But . . . "

"All right, I'll go first." Marina walked onto the stone platform in front of the statue, turned around to face it, and closed her eyes. Carter could see her mouth moving as she spoke to the giant figure in front of her. Then she opened her eyes and walked back to him. "Your turn," she said.

He felt a little silly, but he walked across to the space in front of the statue. What in the world, he thought, was he, the ambassador of the United States of America, doing playing at some kind of voodoo far above the city of Rio de Janeiro?

"Go on," Marina said.

Carter looked up and closed his eyes. He loved her. It might be silly, but was it too much to do something like this for the woman he loved? For someone who loved him, who had never loved anyone else but him? He paused for a moment, then opened his eyes. "I've forgotten the questions," he said.

Marina smiled at him. "No, you didn't," she said. "The statue answered them already."

They had dinner at a small northeastern restaurant in Santa Teresa. "Let's go to Siqueira Campos," Carter said as they finished a super-sweet coconut dessert.

"No," Marina said, "Let's go somewhere different. There's a small hotel a couple of kilometers down the road from here. It's really nice, and it's got a wonderful view. Let's go there."

"Did you ever go there with one of your clients?"

Marina wrinkled her face into a grin. "Oh, don't be so silly, Tony," she said. "You know the answer to that question. This isn't the same. Come on, let's go."

The Hotel Paineras was perched on an outcropping of rock only a hundred meters below the top of Corcovado itself. A large picture window looked from their room out over the Lagoa and Ipanema and Leblon beyond.

Marina stood in front of it. "Look, how lucky, Tony," she said. "The last room in the hotel. You know what I want to do?" She dashed for the bathroom. "I'll show you," she said.

Marina was stark naked when she emerged from the bathroom and ran back over to the window. "I want all of Rio de Janeiro to see how much I love you," she said, "and how much you love me. I want them to see us making love." She opened the blinds of the window, which looked out over the city. "Take off your clothes," she ordered, "and sit down on the bed."

Carter did as he was told. Marina walked over in front of the view and spread her arms and her legs. "Look at us, Rio de Janeiro, we are in love," she shouted. She turned and sat down on his lap and wrapped her legs around him before she brought him inside her. She kissed him, her tongue working its way first through his lips, then to his ear. "Slowly," she whispered, "I want it to last forever."

It was the sound of an insistent "Caw! Caw! Caw!" that woke him just as the sun was rising. A macaw, a great flash of blue and red feathers, sat on a branch a few meters below the window, greeting the dawn. To his left, Carter could see the huge statue of Christ still standing on the summit of Corcovado. There was no sign of an atomic cloud behind it. More than one thousand meters below him lay the city of Rio de Janeiro, waking to the brilliant sun of another tropical day. No cloud of radioactive dust was anywhere to be seen. No destruction. No sign of nuclear war. . . . It wasn't going to happen. It was only April 1, but he knew it wasn't going to happen.

"Are you thinking again?" Marina's voice came from the bed behind him.

"Yes," he said, "but not about the coup. About the statue. And about the macaw."

At that moment, the bird squawked again, still louder than before.

"Is he your macaw?" Marina asked.

"No."

"But I am your lover. Come back to bed."

It was an order he could not refuse.

CHAPTER 35

Carter dropped Marina off at Siqueira Campos. "I'll pick you up for dinner about nine," he said. "It's a nice place. You're going to like it."

"Where? I need to know how to dress."

"It's a surprise," Carter said. "You can dress any way you want. You'll be the most beautiful woman in the place no matter what you wear."

Carter decided to drive along Avenida Atlantica on his way to the office. Although it was early by Brazilian standards, the beach was already full of gorgeous young girls, toasting in the sun, handsome young men playing volleyball, a few older folks relaxing on their beach chairs. There were beach vendors everywhere, stamping through the sand and selling everything from soft drinks, beer, ice cream and crackers to suntan lotion, hats, balloons, and hippie jewelry. No one seemed to care whether there had been a coup, and if so, how it had come out.

"Good morning, boss," Joannie said when Carter arrived at the office. "Welcome to the battlefield."

"What battlefield?"

"Well, April Fool! It's not exactly a battlefield. Looks like everybody got together for a big party over in front of the Ministry of War. They're waiting now for General Amaral to arrive. They say he left Juiz de Fora about four thirty yesterday afternoon". She grinned. "Looks like you were lucky to catch him in Juiz de Fora before he left."

"Let's keep that between us," Carter said. "Has Washington been informed of what's going on?"

"Yes, sir. General Werner thought it would be helpful to send a cable since you weren't here. He'd like to see you when you have a moment."

"All right. Ask him to come over in fifteen minutes. Anything else?"

"Yes, Ambassador Sverdlov invited you to lunch at one o'clock."

"Lunch?"

"Yes, sir."

"Today?"

"Yes."

"Call and tell him I accept," Carter said. "With pleasure. And get me a bottle of champagne from the commissary, the best they've got. Chilled, if possible."

General Werner strode into Carter's office precisely fifteen minutes later. His limp was almost gone. "Well, Tony," Werner said, "it looks like it's all coming together just the way it should."

"You mean the generals won," Carter said.

"Well," Werner said, "let's put it this way: Democracy is being restored."

"April Fool," Carter said softly.

"What's that?"

"Never mind," Carter said. "Anything else?"

"Jango is on his way out of the country."

"Your people didn't try to shoot him?"

Werner looked hurt. "My people?" he said. "Harry is the CIA station chief. You know that. That's his agency's job. Ask him. My job is military attaché."

"I'm not sure what I know, Otto. If you are CIA, of course you'll deny it. They say the only way you can be sure anyone is a CIA agent is if he denies it."

Werner remained silent for a moment. "The one big pity," he said, "is that Brother Sam never happened. Washington ordered it stopped one hundred miles offshore. It would have been a real lesson to all of Latin America if it could have been here to support the revolution and demonstrate our commitment to democracy. We only missed it by a day. If Amaral hadn't started down from Juiz de Fora yesterday afternoon, Brother Sam would have been here when the revolution went off. I wonder what got Amaral started early Tony. Any ideas?"

"You know, Otto," Carter said, "maybe I'm CIA, too. Of course, I deny it."

Werner laughed. "Touché, Mr. Ambassador," he said.

"There is one more thing," Werner continued. "At this point, it's probably better to keep Brother Sam's existence secret. Since it wasn't needed, we turned it around this morning while it was still at sea. You wouldn't want the Commies telling the world that we were about ready to invade. Too much good propaganda for them in that."

"Invade?"

Werner paused. "Wrong word. I should have said 'lend our support.'"

"Yes, but you said 'invade.' Like I asked you long ago: How many aircraft, Otto? How many troops?"

"I can't tell you that, Tony. Washington wants the whole operation kept secret. It never happened. It simply never happened."

"How far did Brother Sam get?" Carter asked.

"How far?"

Carter nodded.

"We turned it around roughly one hundred nautical miles east of Rio."

"In Brazilian waters?"

"As far as I know, yes," Werner said. "Why do you ask?"

"Just curious," Carter said.

Ambassador Sverdlov was waiting just inside the front door of the Soviet embassy residence when Carter arrived.

"Anthony," the Russian said, giving Carter a suffocating bear hug, "How good of you to come." He stopped suddenly. "You know," he said, "we are supposed to be enemies, not friends. People must not see us." He laughed.

"If you wish, I can curse you out for the cameras every so often," Carter said.

"Next week we can go back to that," Sverdlov said, "but not today. Today we celebrate."

Carter followed the Russian down a marble corridor into the study. The walls, some twelve feet high, were covered in a dark green velvet, set off at the ceiling and the floor by an ornate molding painted in gold leaf. On the burnished Brazilian hardwood floor were several exquisite Chinese carpets with animals woven into them. The glass doors on one wall opened onto a carefully tended garden. Two other walls held a collection of a Di Cavalcanti, two Picassos, a Chagal, and a pair of portraits by a Russian painter Carter did not recognize. The last wall held a hardwood bookshelf. The books, all of them leatherbound, were in Russian, English, French, German, and a few in Portuguese. Several French provincial chairs, upholstered in red silk that perfectly matched the carpet, were scattered around the room. A large leather sofa and two easy chairs were clustered around an English coffee table on which sat a small can of caviar, small dishes of chopped egg and chopped onions, and a basket of crackers. Next to the tray was a bottle of clear liquid.

"Sit down, sit down, Anthony," Sverdlov said. "I'm so glad you were free."

"For you, Ivan, I would make myself free no matter what. We deserve to celebrate. In fact, I brought you a bottle of champagne."

Sverdlov looked at the bottle. "Perrier Jouet, 1961. That's very nice of you, Anthony. I'll put it on ice. It will be nicely chilled by the time we get to the fish course. But first, we are going to have some of the finest Russian vodka ever made and some good Iranian caviar. I've been saving them, Anthony, for just such an occasion as this."

The vodka and the caviar were indeed superb and by the time they moved to the dining room for the soup course, Carter was already high.

"I hope you like borscht," Sverdlov said. "I know that borscht is somewhat plebian, but this is Ukrainian borscht. My cook is from the Ukraine via Paris. Borscht is her specialty."

Carter assured him that he adored a good borscht, although he had never had borscht, good or bad. In fact, it was good, very good.

"I'm so glad you liked it," Sverdlov said. "Did you really like it or are you just saying so to be polite?"

"I loved it," Carter said.

The Russian was delighted.

The fish course was a filet of sole, perfectly sautéed and served in a champagne butter sauce with a touch of salmon caviar, accompanied by Carter's bottle of champagne.

"The perfect accompaniment, Anthony," the Russian said happily. "Like a good pianist accompanying Mirnov." Carter had no idea who Mirnov was, but he effusively agreed.

The best and final course was a golden brown crackling duck in orange sauce, served over thin slivers of slightly browned potatoes, bordered by red cabbage and sautéed garlic. It was accompanied by a bottle of 1958 Chateau Margaux, which combined perfectly with the duck.

Lunch was over, and Sverdlov picked up a wooden box on his desk. "Come, Anthony," he said. "Let us have some cigars before we go on to dessert. They're Cohibas, Fidel's favorite." Carter followed him onto the terrace outside the study.

"That was magnificent, Ivan," Carter said. "Just magnificent." The Russian beamed. "But may I ask you a question?" Carter continued, as he sat down.

"Of course."

"Ivan . . . "

"Go on."

"You won't be offended?"

"No, I won't."

"You're sure?"

"Yes, I'm sure. In fact, I think I know what your question is. Would you rather I ask it?"

"That would be very kind," Carter said.

"All right. You want to know how a good Soviet Communist such as I can put on a meal such as this for an American ambassador such as you."

Carter nodded.

"Well, because it's probably the last truly good meal I shall ever have in life and it is fitting that I have it as a celebration with you. You see, the embassy has all the good ingredients and great wines that we need to put on a great meal if we need to for a truly distinguished visitor. And that, my friend, is what you are today."

"That is very kind, Ivan, but what have I done to make me so distinguished?"

The Russian looked over at him through the haze of his cigar. "You caused the coup to happen two days earlier than planned, so I was able to tell the Kremlin that the coup happened before Brother Sam entered Brazilian waters, so there was no reason to sink it."

"How do you know I did that, Ivan?"

"You can't expect me to answer that, Mr. Ambassador," the Russian said, a twinkle in his eye. "We don't engage in espionage. We don't even have any intelligence agents here."

"So you told the Kremlin that Brother Sam never entered Brazilian waters? How could you do that? Your submarines must have known where the flotilla was."

Sverdlov looked nervously over his shoulder. Then he stood up and closed the door into the house. "No, Anthony," he said, "it was not true. The *Forrestal* entered almost one hundred miles into Brazilian waters."

Carter stared at him. "Then why didn't Premier Kruschev order your submarines to sink it?"

"Because I lied to him. I told him that the Brazilians only claimed a twelve-mile territorial sea. That used to be true. But now it is two hundred miles. The premier didn't know that the *Forrestal* had sailed almost one hundred miles into what were actually Brazilian waters.'"

Carter couldn't speak.

"And that is the reason why this was probably the last good meal I shall ever have," Sverdlov said. "In the Soviet Union, you do not eat well after you have lied to the premier, if you eat at all. Come, let us go inside and have dessert. Floating Island. It is very good."

Carter was still somewhat drunk when he arrived back at the embassy.

"How was lunch, boss?" Joannie said.

"Very good, and very sad."

"Why sad, boss?"

"I'd rather not talk about it," Carter said.

"Well, this will cheer you up: There's a cable from the White House, the president wants to see you. I've booked you a seat in first class on Pan Am tomorrow night."

Better to meet with LBJ, Carter thought, than with Kruschev. He would not want to be in Sverdlov's shoes. But Marina wasn't going to be happy.

"OK," Carter said. "But for tonight, please get me a reservation in the main dining room at the Copacabana Palace. And tell Joaozinho I'll need him tonight."

"Yes, boss," she said.

"I'm going out to H. Stern," he said. "What's a nice stone to go on light brown skin?"

"I don't have light brown skin," Joannie said.

"Come on," Carter said. "I need your help."

"OK," Joannie said, "an aquamarine. I like tourmalines myself."

CHAPTER 36

It was, as the night manager of the Copacabana Palace Hotel was to tell his grandchildren many years later, the most unforgettable night of his entire career. It was April 1, the night of the coup of 1964, he remembered. Anthony Carter, the United States ambassador to Brazil, arrived at the hotel in his Cadillac limousine a little after nine o'clock, accompanied by Marina.

The manager knew Marina, of course. She was far and away the most attractive of all the call girls who visited the hotel from time to time to visit its wealthy American or European clients. The manager himself had called on her services for the sultan of Oman not that long ago. The sultan had been entirely satisfied, and had tipped the night manager handsomely. Marina was always respectful, always friendly, never rude to any of the staff. In fact, everyone loved her. It's just that they couldn't afford her.

And so Athaide, the rotund night doorman, had welcomed her as if she were visiting royalty. "How wonderful to see you, Marina," he said with a smile that was entirely genuine. "And you, too, Mr. Ambassador. You are a lucky man to be so well accompanied." Athaide knew everyone worth knowing in Rio de Janeiro, and all the ambassadors, whether they were worth knowing or not. Carter was definitely worth knowing. "Come in, come in," he said as he ushered them

through the door. "It's much cooler inside." He handed them politely
to the night manager and returned to his post outside.

The night manager was surprised to see the American ambassador at the hotel again, this time with Marina. He had been there
just a few days before with a cute American blonde and had signed
in as Wyman Stone. And now he was there with Marina. And what
a Marina! She had on a deep blue silk shantung dress cut just deep
enough for the night manager to skip a breath. In her cleavage hung
a perfect teardrop aquamarine, gleaming against the darkness of
her skin. Two tiny aquamarines sparkled at her ears as well. On her
feet were a pair of blue patent leather pumps with three-inch stiletto
heels. She wore no makeup except for some soft light pink lipstick. In
short, she glowed. She looked to the night manager like the storybook
young wife of the American ambassador to the Federative Republic
of Brazil, as close to royalty as you could get. She almost was.

The night manager escorted the royal couple into the dining
room and delivered them to the maître d'hôtel. Their table was waiting; the best table in the restaurant, looking out a front window to the
sea, with a simple white candle lit—and three red roses in a small
crystal vase. The maître d'hôtel hurried away and returned with two
flutes of champagne, "courtesy of the management," he said to Marina.
Carter might just as well not have been there.

There were several people in the restaurant who Carter knew.
He nodded politely in the direction of the head of the Ag Section of
USAID, having dinner with his overweight wife. The deputy director of USIS was also there with a more attractive wife (perhaps
not his own). Gabriel Ferreira, the AMFORP attorney who had
invited him and Priscilla to the Carnaval parade, and his lovely
wife Eliana, were seated across the room. Carter signaled for them
to come over.

"Gabriel, Eliana" he said, "may I introduce you to my friend . . . "
for a fraction of a second, the name "Yemanja" ran through his brain.
"Marina," he said.

The Ferreiras greeted her warmly, asked where she was from, and complimented her on the aquamarines. "Oh," Marina said, a twinkle in her eye. "I come from the sea. That's why I am wearing aquamarines. Tony gave them to me. Aren't they lovely?"

Ferreira looked at her again. There was something familiar there. Had he seen her somewhere before? But he couldn't bring her into focus.

Lemonov, the Romanian ambassador, came into the dining room about ten o'clock, accompanied by a call girl who Marina knew professionally. Either they did not recognize her, or they ignored her, as the etiquette of the street required.

Dinner was fabulous. Perhaps not quite as good as Ivan's Ukrainian cook could produce, but close. They started with creamed wild mushroom tart, then went on to a medium rare slice of beef Wellington with scalloped potatoes and crisp green beans, and for dessert a superb mousse of maracuja. They drank champagne all the way through, except for a half bottle of 1961 Chateau Lafite Rothchild to go with the beef. They were both quite drunk by the time the coffee came.

"Oh, Tony, that was wonderful! The food, the hotel, all the people who saw me with you. I'm so proud. And tomorrow you'll come out to the factory, and I'll introduce you to everyone there! That's going to be such fun. I love you so much."

This moment had been coming, Carter knew, but he couldn't figure out what he could do about it. He had no choice but to fly to Washington tomorrow. He had put off telling her for as long as he could, but in the end there was nothing he could do but tell her the truth. "I can't, darling," he said. "I have to go to Washington. The president wants to see me."

"Tomorrow?"

"Yes. I have to go tomorrow. I won't be gone long."

"And your politician president is more important than me?" The tears were starting to well up in her eyes. "Until today I had to compete with our generals. Well, today is April 1 and I beat them. And now I'm supposed to compete with your president? I can't do it anymore, Tony. I just can't."

Carter remained frozen to his seat as Marina got up and ran toward the door of the restaurant. A large tray of glasses and dirty dishes stood by the door. She stopped, turned and glared back at Carter. "No more," she said. She lifted the tray from one side and sent an avalanche of glasses, dishes, and silverware crashing onto the floor. Then she straightened her back and strode out of the room.

The night manager gazed in the direction of Marina's *bunda*. "Magnificent," he said to himself. "Simply magnificent."

CHAPTER 37

Harry sat in the back of the plane in seat 32C. He didn't care that he was in tourist class. He was short enough that the legroom was enough. And since he didn't believe in lucky or unlucky numbers, he couldn't have cared less what row he was in. Although passengers in the rear of the plane were supposed to board first, he had waited until he saw Carter come aboard and disappear into the first-class cabin. He wasn't interested in talking with Carter about the attempted kidnapping, or anything else either.

Well, he thought, the Agency had truly screwed up this time. The kidnapping had really been Otto's plan, but he had provided Otto with the information he had requested as well as one of the cars. It wasn't completely an Agency operation, but it certainly was involved.

And then there were the photos of Carter and Marina. What good had they been? He had sold them to the Russians for $10,000, but as far as he could tell, the Soviets had not used them at all. The Agency hadn't used them either. Why had he bothered?

The biggest screw up had to be Brother Sam. How could the Agency have sent that fucking flotilla to Brazil so late that it hadn't even appeared in Guanabara Bay when Amaral arrived in Rio? In fact, they now were saying that Brother Sam was supposed to arrive two weeks after the coup. Harry snorted. How was that for incompetence? They had to be lying through their teeth.

And then there was Jango. That wasn't incompetence. Carter had simply outfoxed him. He was just as glad. He enjoyed shooting, but he didn't much like killing people, even a pinko like Goulart. He hadn't much enjoyed killing that lawyer either. Now that was bad luck, the kid's bad luck. If he just hadn't come home for lunch, it wouldn't have happened. But he did. He had left Harry no choice. Harry was sorry about that, but that's the way it was.

Four operations, Harry thought, the photos, the kidnapping, the assassination, and Brother Sam. Four fuckups! And now they were reassigning him to Chile, maybe to shoot some pinko president there. Only next time, Harry thought, I won't miss . . . unless maybe I want to.

The stewardess was saying something about life jackets when Harry decided that he wasn't going to Chile. There was a shooting school for kids out in Fairfax County, Virginia, run by a friend of his at the NRA. Maybe he would call him when he arrived in Washington. He certainly knew how to shoot. He was sure he could teach some kids.

Carter settled back in his leather seat in first class. He deserved first class. It was he, after all, who had persuaded Amaral to start the revolution—the coup—before Brother Sam would arrive in Rio. Thanks to Carter, the coup had happened first, on March 31. Brother Sam had turned around on April 1, before it reached Rio, before Kruschev would order his submarines to sink the American ships. Ivan should be sitting there, too. Without Ivan, Carter would not have known where the flotilla was at the critical moment. And Kruschev would have known that Brother Sam had already penetrated Brazilian waters.

For the first time in recent history, Carter thought, representatives of the United States and the Soviet Union had worked together to avert a world disaster. And it was he—Carter—who had prevented the Agency from assassinating yet another president. He had served his country well.

Carter accepted a glass of champagne from the passing stewardess, and raised it in a toast to himself. How, he wondered, might the government reward his accomplishments? Might they push Mahon aside and appoint him assistant secretary of state? Or perhaps ambassador to an important European country? London? Paris? Or maybe NATO? In the end it would be the president's call. That had to be the reason they had called him to Washington.

CHAPTER 38

Marina was beside herself. The same supplier who had sent her the winter flannel going into the summer season had now sent her instead a fabric which, although the right weight, was a blend of cotton and polyester. Her order had specified cotton, not a blend. She was sure of that. Did the goddamn supplier think that just because her factory was located in Bangu, she could not tell the difference between one hundred percent cotton and a blend? She bent over to the lower shelf where the purchase orders were kept, and felt a pair of hands on her ass. "Get your hands off me, Jean Pierre!" she snarled.

"I'm sorry, Marina. You are just so delectable that it is hard to resist," the Frenchman said. He sounded a little hurt.

Marina stood up. Jean Pierre looked and smelled a little better than the last time she had seen him. His hair had been cut, his complexion was less pasty, and he seemed to have had a bath. "Oh, I'm sorry, Jean Pierre. I've been having a few problems lately," she said.

"Romantic problems?"

Marina scowled. "No," she said. Jean Pierre looked disappointed. "Fabric problems. Would you care to help?" Her sarcasm was unmistakable.

Jean Pierre smiled. "Perhaps with French fabric," he said.

Marina looked at him, suddenly interested. Wouldn't Mesbla's buyer love some toddler dresses made of French fabric? "Where will I get French fabric?" she asked.

"Why, in France, of course."

Marina was disgusted again. How could men be so stupid? "But I am not in France," she said. "I am in Bangu. And I have to choose my fabrics for myself."

Jean Pierre looked at the gorgeous mulatta afire in front of him. "You could go to France," he said, "with me."

Marina stared at him. "I couldn't afford it. You know I don't work the streets anymore."

"I know. The trip is on me. All of it. I am going to Paris on business. That is why I came over today. To invite you to come along."

"And what do you want in exchange?"

"What do you think?" Jean Pierre said. "It's not your rice and beans."

Marina walked to the office door and looked out at the Women's Penitentiary of Bangu. It wasn't only that institution that kept women imprisoned. It was Bangu itself. Bangu versus Paris. Who would win that soccer game?

Or, how about Bangu versus Washington? Tony hadn't even offered to take her along to Washington. And what was going to happen when Tony was assigned to another embassy somewhere else? Sure, the Copacabana Palace had been great, but would he take a former call girl with him to another post, even if he was in love with her?

Marina turned back to Jean Pierre. "How long would we go for?"

"Oh, not long," Jean Pierre said. "A week or two. Unless you decide you want to stay longer. And I promise to take a bath every other day."

Marina laughed. "I'll think about it," she said.

"Come along," Jean Pierre said. "Please come, April is wonderful in Paris. They even wrote a song about it."

"I said I'll think about it. And I will. But not if you continue to whine at me. So get out of here."

"*À bientôt*," Jean Pierre said. "You are fantastic."

Onilha sat in her pilot's chair, a gift from a French client some years ago, knitting a pink toddler's cap. "Well," she said. "it's a nice offer. No one ever invited me to Paris."

"I know, Momma," Marina said, "but I am in love with Tony, not Jean Pierre."

"How do you know?" her mother said.

"I just know," Marina said.

"And what do you think is love?"

"I don't know that."

"Well, if you don't know what it is, how can you know whether you are in it?"

Marina remained silent.

"You remind me of when you were six. You didn't like spinach, although you had never had any. Isn't this the same thing, just backwards?"

Marina shrugged. "You're right, Momma," she said. "But I still think I love him."

"Even if he doesn't love you?"

There was a long silence. Onilha laid down her knitting. "Where is your ambassador now?" she asked.

"I told you. He's in Washington."

"When is he coming back?"

"I don't know."

"The trip to Paris, if you go, is tomorrow?"

"Yes."

"And when would you come back?"

"One or two weeks."

Another silence. "Why can't you go to Paris on a little trip with the Frenchman," Onilha asked, "even if you are in love with your ambassador?"

"But if I am in love with him, how can I go off to Paris with some-one else?"

"Why not? Isn't that just what your clients did when you were working? Not all of them, but I'm sure a lot of them loved their wives while they were fucking you. That surely was true of a lot of my clients, and I'm sure men haven't changed that much over the years.

"All right, you've fallen in love with one of your clients. That happens to a lot of girls. But that doesn't mean they don't fuck anyone else. Of course they do. The only difference with you is that you get a trip to Paris instead of getting money. Sounds like a pretty good deal to me."

Carter sat on one of the three spindly chairs in the hall outside the Oval Office. Surprisingly, there was no one else except for a nasty-looking Secret Service agent standing next to the door. The corridor where the chairs were located was entirely plain, except for three paintings of George Washington, one of them the famous picture of Washington crossing the Delaware.

He should have brought Marina with him, he thought. He missed her. Life without her was not a whole lot of fun.

The door swung open. "Anthony," the president's voice boomed, "come in, come in, boy. So nice of you to come. Sit down, sit down." The president steered him to the sofa he had seen so often on TV and in the press. "Did you have a good trip?" Carter had no time to reply. "That's good, that's good." The president said. "So what's the situation in Brazil?"

"Well, sir," Carter said, "Marshal Braga seems to be firmly in control. He has assured us that power will be returned to civilian control in several months, after the Communists have been cleared out."

"Goulart?"

"As far as I know, on his way to Uruguay."

"And Brother Sam?"

Carter was surprised. "I don't know, sir. I was mostly out of the loop. I believe it has turned around and is returning home, but you would be better informed by Admiral Whitcroft."

The president snorted. "That idiot!" he said. "He couldn't find

Brazil if he were sitting on it." He looked at Carter. "You know I authorized that operation?"

"Yes, sir."

"And I told you to keep out of it."

"Yes, sir, but . . . "

The president cut him off. "No 'buts,' Anthony. The buck stops with me. I'm the commander in chief. I can't let anyone countermand my decisions without my consent, just like you couldn't let anyone in the embassy countermand yours."

"There was a risk of nuclear war, sir."

"I am aware of that," the president snapped. "That was also my department, not yours. And so was the elimination of President Goulart. I'm sort of glad it failed, but his elimination was my decision to make, not yours."

"I'm sorry, sir. I was unaware that you had authorized that operation. But in any case, I could not agree to the assassination of a democratically elected president, whether of another country or our own. Like I said, I didn't know you had authorized it. But even if I had known, I would have done what I could to prevent it . . . or I would have resigned."

The president gazed at him. "You're a gutsy son of a bitch," he said. "I was going to fire your ass. But I think I'll let you take early retirement. That way you can get your benefits. Now, get the hell out of here before I change my mind." The president stood up. "Good luck, Tony." he said as he steered Carter out the door.

Carter sat in the same first class seat as he had on the flight to Washington. What the hell, he thought, he hadn't retired yet. On the seat next to him lay an envelope containing his divorce papers, which he planned to review on his way to Rio. He had no idea what he would do next; whatever it might be, he would stay in Brazil with Marina.

The flight was uneventful. He moved quickly through the

immigration line at Galeao and got into a bright yellow taxi. "Siqueira Campos," he said to the driver. "Let's go via Avenida Atlantica."

It was more than twenty years since the first time he made that trip. The favelas along the way had grown a bit, the motels were mostly the same (although now he knew what they were for), the Copacabana Palace was exactly the same—except to him it would never feel the same after his dinner with Marina last week—the same beautiful young girls were on the beach, except that they were the daughters or granddaughters of those he had seen twenty years ago.

The taxi made its way up Figueredo Magalhaes, turned left, and headed down Rua Siqueira Campos. A light was on in Marina's apartment. Carter paid the taxi and bounded up the stairs. He would surprise her, he thought, as he opened the door with his key. Inside, the apartment looked as if someone had left in a hurry. There was a note on the bed.

"Tony," it said. "I am in Paris. I love you—I think. Marina."

ACKNOWLEDGMENTS

With many thanks to:

Mike Morris, my secretary for all these years, who skillfully typed the manuscript of this book and put it into the necessary form, and never charged me even one cruzeiro.

Joan Hunter, who expertly and gently coached me in its completion, and made sure Marina had an important role in it.

Paulinho Rocha, my Brazilian brother, who showed me Rio de Janeiro year by year, and still does.

The beautiful Eliana, Paulinho's sister, who brought me and Susan into her home and made us a part of her family.

Susan, my amazing wife, without whom I could never have written this book, much less put it into final form.

ABOUT THE AUTHOR

Peter Hornbostel is an international lawyer, a writer of short stories, and the Artistic Director of a community theatre in Washington, Virginia. He worked for the United States government in Rio de Janeiro and Washington DC from 1963 to 1968 and started his law practice soon after. He has lived in Rio for six years, and has visited Brazil more than 100 times. He has permanent resident status in Brazil and is an honorary member of the Brazilian Air Force. He lives with his wife in the Blue Ridge Mountains of Virginia.

Also Available from Four Winds Press

Sacred Bones: Confessions of a Medieval Grave Robber by Michael Spring. $14.95, 978-1-940423-10-4. Based on the true story of Deusdona ("God's gift"), a ninth-century Roman deacon who worked in the catacombs digging up worthless bones and selling them off as the holy remains of saints and martyrs.

Apples & Oranges: In Praise of Comparisons by Maarten Asscher. $15.95, 978-1-940423-06-7. Are comparisons across genres inherently invalid, or can they be illuminating? In 22 wide-ranging essays, Dutch author Maarten Asscher maintains that comparisons can be the highest form of argument.

17 Stone Angels: A Novel by Stuart Archer Cohen. $15.95, 978-1-940423-05-0. Crimes of the lowest and highest order come together in Buenos Aires, one of the most dangerous and beautiful cities on earth, when corrupt police chief Miguel Fortunato is assigned to invesitgate a murder he committed.

The Voyage of the UnderGod: A Comedy by Kirby Smith. $14.95, 978-1-940423-02-9. A political satire about charismatic right-winger Luther Dorsey's last grasp for the greatness he thinks he deserves, *UnderGod* tells the tale of a reality-TV tall ship's sailing voyage around Cape Horn.

Laughing Cult: Poems by Kevin McCaffrey. $13.95, 978-1-940423-00-5. A highly accessible collection that combines a quirky sensibility with traditional poetic forms to create miniature sketches marked by romantic ambiguity, occultism, science fiction, and quirky angst.

Invisible World by Stuart Archer Cohen. $15.95, 978-1-940423-04-3. An invitation from a dead man propels Chicagoan Andrew Mann to abandon his mundane existence and embark on a perilous journey from Hong Kong to Inner Mongolia in search of a fabled map of the *Invisible World*.

www.fourwindspress.com

CPSIA information can be obtained at www.ICGtesting.com
Printed in the USA
LVOW10s2006280415

436390LV00002B/4/P

9 781940 423111